MW01233739

The Crusader

Supervising Editor: L. Austen Johnson
Associate Editors: Sydney Valdens, Chrysa Keenon

www.GenZPublishing.org
Aberdeen, NJ

ISBN (hardcover): 9780997577631
ISBN (paperback): 9781731089175

To Hannah
Anyone can be a Hero.
Hope you enjoy!

THE CRUSADER

Nicholas Chimera

GenZ
The Future of Publishing

6-01-19

To Hannah,
Anyone can be a Hero.
Hope you enjoy!

9-01-16

"Nearly all men can stand adversity, but if you want to test a man's character, give him power."

– Abraham Lincoln

TABLE OF CONTENTS

THE CRUSADER

Prologue

Isabelle Thompson
Supervising engineer on *NAVIGATO* Project
Cape Canaveral Air Force Station, Florida
May 10th, 1969

When high ranking USAF and NASA administrators ask you to supervise an off books project, you don't tell them no. Once Gemini ended, I assumed they'd transfer me to work on Apollo; instead, they transferred me to a project I didn't know existed—

NAVIGATO. They told me two things when I accepted the offer: "Don't ask other people on the project what their job is," and "Never tell anyone what you do." I gave them my word I'd keep those secrets. And for the first two years I upheld that promise.

In 1968 *NAVIGATO* added two new members to the team—Colonel John Wilkins and Lieutenant Colonel Richard Wilde. The two of them flew reconnaissance missions in soviet airspace in the SR-71 Blackbird. The higher ups chose the two of them because they had experience flying the world's fastest aircraft. They had the highest pilot clearances and my bosses assumed if anyone could handle the *NAVIGATO* it was them.

The *NAVIGATO* mission was chartered to construct a rocket capable of flight speeds faster than what the laws of physics account for. The project is only possible because of some undisclosed power source that only one person has access to. I've passed Mr. Akashi in the halls, and he always has the same cold look on his face carrying that containment briefcase around.

Eight months ago I developed a relationship with one of the pilots, Lieutenant Colonel Wilde. This was obviously a breach of protocol, and soon after, the dominoes fell. Richard is one of the very few who actually get to see the ship. Everything changed when Richard told me another division installed slots on the *NAVIGATO* for missiles. I was ordered to design a ship that would launch into space and fly to the moon faster than you could turn on a light switch. The *NAVIGATO* was meant to explore and they turned my ship into a weapon.

I should have expected something like this when they moved operations to the cape instead of Mission Control at Kennedy Space Center. We're ten days from launch and my actions, while noble in origin, may have catastrophic consequences for the entire world. I feel like I've created a monster, and I'm the only one on this project willing to risk everything to figure out what the true purpose of *NAVIGATO* is.

I've taken a huge risk alone by creating this written account of the project. If I fail to stop this catastrophe, I hope someday my notes are recovered. Maybe no one will ever see what I've written. But maybe my transcription of these events will serve as a sign of hope when it's all over, to show that in the darkest hours a few wholesome individuals with love in their hearts can change history.

NICHOLAS CHIMERA

Chapter 1

Chicago, Illinois

2019

Tuesday

2:55 P.M.

"Get off of him!" I yell out to Trey, who holds Daniel Grey up against a locker.

"Screw off, Pat," Trey spits at me tauntingly.

I grab Trey's shoulders and try to pull him off of Daniel. He elbows me in the face. My front foot trips over my back leg and the strike pushes me into the opposite locker. I can barley fling my hands up fast enough to guard my head from impact.

Trey drops my friend and walks towards me—I guess I'm his new target. I clutch the left side of my face and hold back the throbbing pain in my upper cheek.

Before he gets close enough for another elbow, I hit Trey with a front kick in his chest. I press my foot into his gut, forcing him away to create distance.

Trey laughs at my failed attempts to fight him. Without much effort, he throws his weight into a long, arching punch, hitting me square in my left side. I'm so focused on blocking his right hand I don't notice the left hook until it blasts across my face.

I fall straight to the ground, my shoulder digging into the tile floor. My ears ring for a few seconds. I shake it off and push myself up onto my feet. I look up and see Daniel charging at Trey, clutching his pen. But, Daniel stops in his tracks at the sound of the Dean's voice.

"Stop this right now! Trey, one more outburst like this, and you're done at this school," the Dean exclaims.

The Dean grabs Trey by his collar and pulls him away in the direction of his office. I stand up and see Daniel put the pen back into his pocket. Thank God the Dean interrupted, or else Dan might have done something terrible. As I walk toward Daniel, he says to me,

"Thanks for the help Pat. Trey's a real piece of shit."

"Yeah—I just can't believe he beat me. I always assumed I could take anyone in a fight," I say to Daniel.

"You do have a black belt. It's not that out of line to think you could take Trey in a fight," Daniel responds.

"I thought size didn't matter. I guess it does," I say to myself more than Daniel.

"Thanks for the help Pat," Daniel tells me, his shoulders shrinking closer to his centerline.

"Why were you guys even fighting?" I inquire, stepping closer to him.

"I'd rather not talk about it," he responds meekly.

"We don't talk much about anything anymore."

"Well, you know, I've got my stuff and you've got your stuff. We're busy."

"As soon as track settles down we'll hang out, just like we used to."

"Sure," Dan says with disappointment, attempting to hide his doubt with a short smile.

18

3:10 P.M.

Dan walks to his locker, and I walk down to mine at the end of the hall. Taking a deep breath to calm down the adrenaline rush from the fight, I think about how miserable the aesthetic of this place is. The walls not lined with lockers are painted beige and white. The smudged off-white floor tiles make me feel as filthy as they are.

I used to look forward to hanging out with Dan after school, but I never have the time with homework and late college applications. Just a couple more months and I'll be an adult.

I look to my right and see a sophomore trudging through the hallway, carrying a stack of books and loose papers tall enough to cover the boy's chin. He barely makes it to his locker before all his belongings pile onto the floor.

As I walk past the bathroom, I look at the clock above the door. I want to help the kid with his books, but I can't—I'm late for track. I gather my own books and sprint to the football field. Leaving my backpack under the stands, I immediately start running with the others and hope that Coach doesn't notice how late I am.

As usual, practice ends with a 400-meter race—one lap around the field. For the first hundred meters, I hold second, but around the 300-meter mark I fade off to the end of the line.

Practice comes to a finish, and we stretch in the middle of the football field. I lie down on the turf, pushing my upper body down and using my toes as leverage to pull myself closer to my leg. My knee shakes. I lift my leg up slightly to scratch the underside of my shin.

Coach addresses the team.

"Now, guys, listen up. I get your grades from your teachers on Thursday, and if you're not doing well, you can't come to the meet on Saturday. And Patrick Knight?" I raise my head to the call of my name. "I need to talk to you alone."

I stand up, and we walk to the bleachers away from the rest of the team. I follow behind my coach and stop when he turns around. The setting sun shines between the bleachers and I squint my eyes.

"Pat, listen, I don't know if I can let you come to the meet on Saturday."

"Coach, my grades are better than anyone else on the team. I'm taking honors and AP classes," I say.

"I know that Pat, but this isn't an academics problem. The issue is athletics. You can barely keep up with these guys," Coach Molenda says.

"But Coach...."

"It's not your fault, Pat. Most of these guys have been on the team since freshman year."

"I can run a mile in eight minutes. That's the criteria to be on the team," I tell him.

"You can run a mile alright, but when we start talking about two or three miles, you burn yourself out too quickly. I'm just saying, you might want to think about helping the team in a different way."

"Like what?"

"Well, we could use a manager."

"Oh come on, coach!"

"It's important work. We need the help setting up equipment and updating the player stats. You'll still be able to come to meets, and—"

"I love running Coach. I'm not quitting. I know I'm not strong enough for throwing and I can't sprint as fast as most of the others. Distance is the only event I know I can be an important part of.... I promise I'll get better."

"Okay Pat, I'll give you your shot. Maybe next time we can see how you handle high jumps, or maybe hurdles instead. But listen, it's up to you to put in the work."

Coach Molenda walks off. Just as he leaves, I mutter under my breath,

"I do put in the work."

9:45 P.M.

I throw my pencil across the room in a spurt of rage. I cup my face into my hands and let out a sigh. When I finally gain the courage to look at what I've done, I hold up my fifteen-page history outline. I've worked on this monster of an assignment since dinner.

I close my eyes and think about what the rest of my night holds. When I came home, I ate dinner and dove straight into Chapter 19: *The Ferment of Reform and Culture, 1790-1860*. Now, I still need to make flashcards conjugating French Verbs, cut out eighteen triangles and glue them into one triangle, and write a draft for a paper about how I "sympathize" with a character I don't relate to from a book I don't have time to read. And with all of this, the only thing I can truly concentrate on is my rampant desire for sleep.

My head might explode if I work without taking at least a five minute break, and despite the relief that outcome would award me, I give into my instinct for liberation. I walk downstairs and see my dad sitting in the living room watching the news. I decide to join him.

My dad sits comfortably on the brown leather sofa, screwing the cap onto his bottle of water. I walk in silently for some reason. My dad's eyes seem magnetized to the screen. I walk ahead at a normal pace and plop down next to him. I look at him as he watches the television. I turn my head and listen.

The newscasters report that NASA recently came out and disclosed the details of a classified mission they ran during the cold war. They called it the *NAVIGATO* mission, where they tested out a ship they believed could travel faster than the speed of light.

NASA undertook the mission in secret because they feared another public disaster following some of the early Apollo missions, but, nonetheless, a disaster is exactly what happened. They lost contact with the astronauts and are officially disclosing their deaths to the public...fifty years later.

"What do you think about that, Pat?" my dad asks.

"I don't know. I guess I'm not really surprised that the government covered something like that up," I respond to my dad. "What do *you* think happened to those astronauts?"

"Not sure. Maybe they were abducted by aliens," he says with an infectious grin.

"Come on, Dad." We both laugh.

"Faster than the speed of light, huh?" my mom says, walking into the room. "You could get pretty far."

"You could go anywhere," I add.

She pauses for a few seconds. Then she continues, "When I was growing up watching shows like Star Trek or The X-Files, I thought a lot about what life on other worlds would be like. Sometimes, the shows scared me, but your grandfather told me not to be scared. He said that alien children watch TV shows about us, and they're scared too."

"I don't want to be scared."

"People are scared of what they don't know. You know how to not be scared of something?" my mom asks.

"How?" I ask.

"You embrace the unknown."

I start up my homework again and finish around midnight. I'm so tired that I go straight to bed without washing my face.

Wednesday
7:30 A.M.

I get out of bed at the same time as always. I shower, eat breakfast, and, as usual, am late for school. As eight o'clock passes, I start running toward school on a route that usually takes about ten minutes to walk.

The morning is surprisingly foggy, and the cold air doesn't burn my lungs as much as I thought it would. I can feel a little sweat drip from the back of my neck as I jog ahead. I pull the strings on my hoodie. The hood tightens over my frozen ears.

My body shifts from side to side as I make my way to school. I grow fatigued and stop to catch my breath. But, the fog thickens. I loose sight of the apartment buildings around me, barely able to see anything now. I walk slower and try to remember the path to school.

Ahead on the sidewalk, I can barely make out the figure of a man. His outlined humanoid shape appears to not be walking, but instead, floating. The fog makes it impossible to discern his features, but he wears all black. My eyes close instinctively as a blinding green light begins to shine through the fog. I open my eyes but they quickly burn from the radiant burst of light.

Everything starts to spin. I bend my legs slightly and faintly reach my hands out from my body for balance. I become so disoriented that I fall to the ground.

9:35 A.M.

I stand up from the cement and check my watch. The time says two hours have passed, which means I already missed first period. I should be in French class right now. The fog has dissipated, and there's no trace of the man from before.

I shiver as a gust of wind passes by. My skin feels abnormally sensitive, like it's made of tissue paper. I clench my fists together and my forearms immediately ache. My shoulders quiver and I shake it off.

I feel generally unharmed and decide I just need to get to school. I could tell my parents or the police later—although I'm not really sure what happened.

I race up the cement stairs to the school, clutching the straps of my backpack. I enter through the front entrance and sprint down the hall too my locker. To my left I see the sophomore gym class playing basketball. To my right I prepare to make an abrupt turn down the main corridor of the school. I sprint forward. My chest convulses.

I nearly slip as my feet pound against the tiles below. I come to a sudden stop at the sound of the Dean's voice. He says the one sentence I was trying so hard to avoid hearing.

"Patrick, come get your late slip."

I close my eyes and grind my teeth together. I walk ahead trying to control my heavy breathing. I approach the Dean's desk and stare at him as he writes my name on the green tardy slip.

"Six late slips warrant a detention, Patrick."

"I...." I attempt to explain myself to the Dean when he interrupts and continues his thought.

"But, I'm sure I miscounted," he says with a serious face. "We can call this one number five."

I take several seconds to realize that he's cutting me some slack.

"Thank you," I say respectfully.

He hands me my "fifth" late slip and I walk off with the green half sheet of paper.

"Pat," the Dean calls out once more, "Good job standing up for your friend yesterday."

I nod and walk on. I finally make it to class and gently set my late slip on the teacher's desk. I walk to my seat with my head down, trying to escape acknowledgment. The teacher gives me plenty of attitude, as is her custom. She chastises me like I'm a child and tells me to act like an adult. She could at least pick one.

Following some laughter from the rest of the class and the teacher saying, "Children, be quiet when teacher is talking," despite the fact that our class can vote in the next election, she goes on with her lesson on reflexive pronouns.

My eyes grow heavier and heavier. The shaking starts again. My legs twitch below my desk and I grab my knees to hold them in place. Saliva builds up in my mouth and I cough a little. My skull feels like it's compressing into my brain and I close my eyes. I can't bring myself to open them and I fall asleep in my seat.

10:27 A.M.

The bell rings. I gasp for breath and quickly turn my head, glancing around the room to see if anyone noticed. I have never fallen asleep in class before, but I couldn't help myself today. It's grounds for a detention, or at least for the teacher to yell at me again. No one notices. *How did the teacher not see me sleeping?* I think about this on my way to history class.

I stop at my locker for my books, where Trey greets me with a dose of revenge. He slaps my books down and stands in front of my locker blocking the way.

"Please move," I say to Trey.

"Screw you, Patty," Trey says as he shoves me.

My head begins to shake uncontrollably, along with my right fist trembling at my side. In a moment of outrage, I lose the ability to control my anger. I grab him by his collar and yell out, "I said, move!"

I throw Trey across the hall and into a locker, shocked by my own feat. I can see Trey bleeding through his shirt across his back as he slides down, leaving a sizeable dent in the locker.

The Dean runs down the hall asking what happened. I feel too overwhelmed to speak. He escorts me to his office and wastes no time giving me a detention slip. He did not cut me the same slack I received this morning.

I can't believe how easy it is to do bad things. I fall asleep in class and no one notices. I'm an hour late for school and only receive a stern look from the Dean. I nearly kill a kid and I have to give up an hour of my Saturday. That's it? Doesn't anyone care about how I threw Trey, a kid nearly twice my size, and left a dent in a steel locker? I care. How did I do that? Does this have anything to do with what happened this morning?

I ask myself questions like this the rest of the day. After the last bell rings, I go to the library to study, but I can't get any work done. I just sit there reflecting. I guess I am stronger than I thought. Why couldn't I summon this strength yesterday?

I sit at a wooden table alone, scribbling on a piece of paper when I remember I have track practice today. I check the time and decide that if I rush, I can still make the race at the end of practice. I change into my running clothes and head to the field.

The team was just about to start. Today, they've set up hurdles. I apologize to Coach for being late and convince him to let me join the race. We start, and I am at the front as usual. Soon, I expect to be in last. But when the 300-meter mark rolls around, I'm not. In fact, when I check over my shoulder, I can't see anyone close to me.

I approach a hurdle and I jump over it. I coast over the metal obstacle and prepare to continue running. But I don't fall—I can't fall down.

Once I finally land, which takes a couple seconds longer than it should, I arrive at the next hurdle. I leap into the air once more and remain in the air even longer this time.

I focus down and land on my feet. I peer over my shoulder and see five obstacles behind me, but I only remember jumping twice.

I come to a complete stop when I realize I now stand behind the rest of the team who had to turn around to see me standing at our starting point. I ran three hundred and fifty meters in about twenty seconds.

I decide I have no other choice but to keep running. So, I run. I run as fast as I can, and I don't slow down. I run home, and when I get there I check the time on my phone. Only three minutes have passed. I just ran a mile in three minutes. I have so much adrenaline and I have to do *something*.

31

During the hurdles I felt like I was flying. Maybe I can fly. I've done things today I never thought I could do. I feel powerful. If I have abilities then I need to tell someone. I can't just sit on the knowledge that I can do incredible things and not share it with anyone else. I have to tell someone.

I grab my phone and call Dan, listening to the dial tone ring twice before he answers.

"Hey Pat, what's up?" Daniel asks, his voice sounding tired

"Dan, I need you to come over to my house. Where are you?" I ask.

"I'm close. I can start walking over now. Be there soon."

Chapter 2

4:45 P.M.

I wait eagerly at home for about five minutes before I hear a delicate knock on my door. I open it and let Daniel in. As soon as he enters, I start talking.

"Dan, I think I have superpowers." He begins laughing. I continue, "Dan, I'm serious. Today at school, I pushed Trey into a locker like the thing was made of paper," I say.

"Good job."

"Dan?"

"Those lockers are like a thousand years old. It would have broken if you leaned on it too hard." Daniel says.

"I ran a mile in three minutes," I tell him.

"That's funny," Daniel responds.

"I'm serious! And I think I can fly," I tell my friend.

"Ha! That's really funny."

"I'm not joking Dan."

"Then show me."

Daniel reaches into his old, avocado-colored backpack and pulls out a Frisbee. He opens my front door and steps out onto the porch. Daniel throws the maroon disk onto the roof of the apartment building across the street and says, "If you can fly, then go get my Frisbee."

"Alright, I will," I tell him.

I begin running toward the building. My hands shake as I run under the pressure of proving my abilities. I cross the street, and as my foot hits the grass on the other side, I leap into the air. I begin to rise higher and higher. I feel relaxed— I feel free. I reach the top of the building and can see the Frisbee. I extend my hand out.

I try to move toward the roof, but I miss. I hit the white, brick wall and slide down. I fall towards the base of the building into a patch of thorn bushes. I can hear the wind pushing my body down. A sharp pain rushes up my right leg. I start to convulse at the base of the building, attempting to push myself up. I give up the pointless effort and look at the black and blue blotches pulsing from my skin as I yell out,

"Dan! Help."

7:49 P.M.

My parents wheel me through the front door. The last hour of lecturing at the hospital has satisfied their need to speak further about my accident. I feel so stupid—the Frisbee was within my grasp. Now, even if I do have powers, I won't be able to use them until my leg heals.

My dad picks me up and lays me on the couch. We put the news on again. They play the same story as yesterday but with more details.

According to the news, the ship NASA launched is called the *NAVIGATO* and it took off in 1969, just before the first moon landing. The ship had two pilots: John Wilkins and Richard Wilde.

My dad sits down in his chair across from the couch. He tries to start up a conversation without making me feel bad about my leg.

"I can't believe it's already been fifty years since the moon landing."

"Not until summer, Dad," I poke fun at him.

"Alright, smart guy." He chuckles.

"Dad?"

"Yeah?"

"I'm sorry I broke my leg."

"Pat, don't apologize. You're the one who has to deal with that pain; your mother and I just hate to see you like this. Just be careful next time, okay?"

"Okay, dad."

"Hey, do remember those stories I used to read you when you were younger? Those, uh, Greek Mythology books."

"Of course. Those were great."

"Remember the story about The Chimaera?" my dad asks.

"Yeah, I think so," I respond. "The lion with the head of a goat and snake as a tail?"

"Yep. It breathed fire and flew with the wings of a dragon."

"That's right. The thing was a beast."

"The Chimaera ravaged towns in Greece, burning them down with its breath and flying away from the ashes when it was all over. Do you remember who stopped it?" he asks.

"Bellerophon. He rode in on the Pegasus and killed the monster."

"That's right. He embraced the unknown, but he didn't do it alone. Every story has a lesson, Pat. You never have to do anything alone. Your mom, brother, and I will always be here for you."

"I love you guys."

"I love you too, Patrick," my dad tells me. "Now, why don't you get some sleep? I want you back on your feet soon."

I smile. My dad approaches me and bends over to hug me. I lift myself up awkwardly to partake in the embrace.

"Do you want me to bring you upstairs?" he asks.

"Nah, that's alright. You can't carry me up and down the stairs every morning and night. I'll sleep down here 'til my leg heals. It's a comfy couch anyway."

"Alright. Sleep well buddy." My dad walks off, but not before leaving me a soft, blue blanket.

I'm going to have plenty of time to catch up on the news thanks to this injury. Honestly, it's a pretty convenient excuse to skip track for a while. I don't know how I'm going to explain to Coach Molenda how I was able to jump through the air for nearly fifty meters without landing and not mention that I can fly. At least...I think I can fly.

Thursday

2:00 P.M.

The boredom of studying European socialism doesn't even compare to the monotony of sitting on a couch all day binging daytime television. I want to use my powers so bad. I can't resist tapping my foot against the cherry-red pillow at the base of the couch. The coolest things that I've accomplished today include solving a Rubik's Cube and clearing the DVR. Absolutely riveting.

I hoped the news would at least keep my mind active, but it's the same thing over and over again. Nothing interesting ever happens near me. All the news occurs hundreds of miles away: war in the Middle East, a serial bank robber in London, and a hospital on fire in Chicago's suburbs?

I know that hospital. The facility is only a half-mile away from my house. I went there yesterday after hurting my leg.

If I didn't break my leg trying to prove I could fly, I'd be able to help. I imagine myself over there saving lives. I stomp my foot to the ground. I feel no pain. I stand up as an angry reflex, and my supposedly "broken" leg holds up my weight. I tear off the cast and glance down at my leg. It's fine. In fact, it feels stronger than ever. Whatever happened to me, it means I can heal fast.

I know I can help out at the hospital—I can be a superhero. I just need a costume. I look through some cabinets in my house and stumble upon a blue tablecloth. I tear it into the shape of a cape. I tuck the end of it into my white long-sleeved shirt.

The cape matches my blue jeans, but it's not enough to be a costume. I need something to cover my face so no one can tell who I am.

2:30 P.M.

I sprint upstairs and grab a black ski mask from the pocket of my winter coat. Unfortunately, it doesn't really match the rest of the costume. I can't spend all my time getting a costume together when people need me.

I fly down the staircase and stumble, catching my footing at the base of the stairs. I look up to the second floor and smile.

I rush out the front door. I take a minute to think about what I'm about to do: I'm going to fly to a hospital and save people from a fire—this is awesome.

I run in the direction of the hospital and practice my flight. I can't stay up for more than six seconds without falling. When I take a leap, I feel like a rocket launching up to the stars, and when I fall, adrenaline rushes to my head like a giant drop on a roller coaster. But for the couple seconds where I'm steady in the sky in defiance of the laws of nature, I feel a quiet sensation of harmony.

I continue on this rhythm of sprinting and leaping into the air until I arrive at the hospital. I reach a large white complex and find crowds of people and fire trucks surrounding the perimeter set up by the emergency responders. I run toward one of the firefighters. His height and build discourages me, but I continue on the path. He looks down at me and says,

"What do you want?"

"I want to help. Who needs to be saved?" I ask the firefighter.

"Get out of here, kid. Leave this to someone who knows what they're doing."

The firefighter brushes me off and runs toward a new fire truck that arrives. I take a breath, trying to calm myself down. He has no idea what I am capable of doing. It's not his fault he ignored me. I'll have to show him. I'll show them all what I can do.

I run to the side of the building past a blockade set up by the firemen. The few people in the crowd not staring at the roaring flames from the hospital fire stare at me. I realize how childish I look in the cape. I'm going to be an adult soon, and here I am playing dress-up.

I won't let their stares prevent me from helping the people in the hospital. I bend my knees and push off the cracked cement. I rise up, higher and higher until I land on the roof. I stand there in a proud pose and look down as the onlookers below gaze at me in astonishment.

A feeling of elation overwhelms me as I come to the realization that I made the jump this time, unlike at the apartment building. I'm getting stronger.

My train of thought is interrupted when the roof collapses in on itself. I fall into the building and use my flight to slowly lower my feet to the ground to avoid crashing. I lower my hands down to my side after having instinctively crossed them out in front of me as a shield.

I now stand on the top floor. My eyes tear up as I squint to see through the smoke. The ski mask covers my mouth and protects me from inhaling too much dust, but smoke builds up in my eyes while debris coats over my clothing.

I shut my eyes and rub them with the palms of my hands to ease the itching. This effort does not hinder the scorching feeling. Astonishingly, I can still see the smoke traveling in the hospital hallways; in fact, I can see even better than before. This can't be possible—my eyes are still closed.

This is a new power, some sort of sonar sense that allows me to see with my eyes closed with 360-degree vision. It's a different feeling than my natural sight. It's not even seeing as much as it is sensing what's around me. I can only make out the rough outline of objects without color. How can I do this?

I make out shapes of two people on the floor below me, so I turn around and run at a window. I jump into the air as if performing a cannonball dive into a pool and throw myself through it. The glass shatters. The sunlight shocks my senses as my eyes open.

I start to fall down outside the building and use my flight to direct my body toward the wall and through the window on the floor below. I arch from one window to the one below it like a boomerang. My shoulder slams through the glass, almost forcing me back out the windowpane. Tiny fragments of glass splinter through my cape and shirt.

I barely find my footing on the shards of glass crackling on the floor beneath my gym shoes. The fire oscillates within the cloud of black smoke consuming the ginger colored floor.

I can tell from prior visits here as well as the small blotches that remain clean that the walls used to be white, but the smoke stains the color into shades of gray and black.

I sense two people in the room next to me. As I wipe the sweat from under my mask, my legs tremble with a burning sensation. I look down and see the end of my cape on fire. I reach my hands up to the back of my neck, grab the cape, and tear it off. I drop the tablecloth and watch the blue fabric quickly set aflame.

The indigo color fades and the fabric crisps like charcoal. Coughing under my mask, my subconscious mind replaces my core train of thought. I remember my parents telling me I was born in this hospital. Is there a chance that I might die here, too?

I refocus and run down to the room where those people are trapped. I reach the room and grab the sizzling, golden door handle. My hand instinctively repels from it. I try to open it again, but some fallen wreckage prevents the mahogany door from swinging open. I walk back a few steps and use my body to ram against it and burst through the door.

I rush through, forcing my left arm into the door. The dense mahogany cracks in half and creates an uproar resembling the sound of a limb breaking.

I enter the room to find two nurses screaming. I must have startled them by running through the door. I crashed through the wreckage, and the heaps of wood and office supplies that blocked their only exit. They run to me.

"Follow me," I say in the deepest voice I can muster. They do as I say, and we run to the same window I flew through about a minute ago.

The window is the safest place to exit the building. I know there's less fire there than probably awaits us down the six flights of stairs we would need to walk down to reach the bottom floor.

As we reach the window, I say to the two nurses, "I can only take one at a time. Who's first?"

"We're not going out the window!" one of them yells.

"Please trust me," I say, even though I realize that they have no reason to put their faith in me, a perfect stranger.

I need to show them they can trust me. I lift my foot onto the window and defy everything a person is taught to believe as I leave the building. I struggle to hold myself up in the air as I reach out my hand to one of the nurses.

"Please trust me," I repeat, with a shaky voice. She hesitates at first, but eventually decides to reach out to me. The pain I feel holding myself in the air resembles the sting of holding a plank. Each tiny muscle in my core tenses to keep me airborne.

I pull the nurse out the window holding her in my arms. I hover down as easily as I can, but it's challenging enough to hold even myself up, let alone another person. I overcome the trembling of my straining body and land on the cracked cement below. Neither of us are harmed. I drop her off by an ambulance and fly up to the other nurse, trying not to notice the dozens of people staring.

At the window again, I reach out my hand to the last nurse. I can hear a subtle puff of air a few doors down the hall. A breach in an oxygen tank attracts entropy. I can feel her hand in mine, and I stare into her hazel eyes as a swarm of fire rushes up from behind her toward the window. The flames engulf her body. A shockwave from the fire sends out a force that breaks my grip with her hand and thrusts me several floors below.

I open my eyes and squint as I look away from the sun down past the royal sky around me. I'm lying on the hood of a fire truck. I awake to the sight of a policeman peeling off my mask. He had only been able to uncover my mouth before waking me up. I push him off and fly. Just fly away.

6:00 P.M.

Washington, D.C.

NASA stellar cartographers have worked to compare old images of distant galaxies to new ones and have uncovered something startling.

After analyzing images taken by the Hubble Space Telescope, NASA scientists believe to have found an unidentified object hurdling towards the Earth at roughly two hundred and fifty thousand meters per second.

This measurement is an unfounded number when it comes to asteroid velocity.

Assuming this is in fact an asteroid, that velocity is nearly double the fastest asteroid speed recorded to date.

It is uncertain at this time what the nature of this object is, but what is undeniable is that the object is of overwhelming size.

Though researchers continue to dispute its origin and composition, NASA and international space agencies have come to unanimously agree that the object is heading on a collision course for Earth and, at its current rate of travel, will arrive soon.

Chapter 3

Friday

2:50 P.M.

"That was you?" Daniel asks in amazement. "That's incredible!"

"I know, right? And you thought I was joking when I told you I had powers," I say to Daniel.

"Well, I guess you're a superhero," Daniel says.

"And you're my trusty sidekick," I tell Daniel.

"What's your superhero name going to be?" Daniel asks.

I shrug. It's not something I've thought about yet.

In response, he says, "It needs to be cool, or else no one will take you seriously."

"Good point." I pause. "How about The Cavalier?"

"What are you, from Cleveland?"

"No, I just like the name."

"I thought you liked The Bulls?"

"I do. I just thought it would be a good name."

"It's no name for a Chicago Bulls fan."

"Fine, then, what do you suggest?" I ask.

"Well, how about the school mascot?" Daniel suggests.

"The Crusader?"

"Yeah, why not?"

"I guess it's kind of cool...Yeah, let's do it. I'm The Crusader!"

"You're the Silent Crusader."

"No. The Chicago Crusader!"

"Don't say it too loud. Someone might overhear us," Daniel says.

We laugh and I continue, "Anyway, can I sleep over at your house on Sunday?" I ask.

"Sure, but don't we have school Monday?"

"No, we have the day off. Teacher meetings or something"

"That's right. Awesome, sounds good. I'll see you then."

"See you later, Dan."

Dan and I go our separate ways. Normally I would be heading to track workouts after school, but I quit the team. I don't want anyone to figure out that I'm The Crusader. Huh...the name is actually growing on me.

3:10 P.M.

I continue walking toward my house. I'm nearly halfway there, walking at a casual pace, when I hear the screeching of tires behind me. I turn my head abruptly and see a jet-black limo pull over on the road beside me. The door kicks open, and a man inside wearing a suit and sunglasses orders, "Get in, kid."

"No. I'd rather not," I say to him.

"Get in, or we tell the world your little secret."

"I don't have any secrets," I say to the man, wondering if he actually knows about my powers.

"How about the secret that you can fly? Or the secret that you—" the man starts to say before I interrupt.

"Fine! I'll come with you," I blurt out in a panic. "Just shut up."

I look around the neighborhood and see no one. I try to weigh my options here. I could run. Heck, I could even fly. But I can't stay up in the air long enough to loose them. These guys could follow me home. I'd be dragging my parents and Kevin into trouble they don't deserve. I could fight these guys, but I don't know who they are. It's not good practice to fight an enemy you're unfamiliar with. I don't even know how many of them there are, and I can't risk getting shot.

If I go with them, there's a better chance this can end without a fight. And, if things go wrong, at least I know I tried to do this the right way.

I enter the car and sit between two suited men and across from three more. I can't see the front seat because of the limo's divider, but it seems safe to assume there are two others up front in the driver's and passenger's seats.

51

I have no clue what they want with me. Maybe they're with the government? I know I need to be prepared to fight my way out of this if it doesn't go well. But for now, I just need to play along and keep it cool.

3:40 P.M.

We drive in the limo for half an hour in complete silence. Looking out the window, I begin to see the outline of the Chicago skyline.

I finally muster enough confidence to speak to the men. I ask the man across from me, "Where are you taking me?"

There is no response.

"How do you know about my powers?"

Once again, the men remain silent and ignore me.

The car pulls up next to a tall, dark building in downtown Chicago. The man who first spoke to me opens the door. The five men riding in the back seat escort me out of the car. As one climbs off of the leather seating of the limo's interior, his suit coat slides back to reveal a gun in a holster on his hip.

I exit the vehicle and walk toward the entrance of the building. The five suited men surround me. I look behind, and the limo drives off. I strap on my backpack and squint up at the reflection of the sun in the windows of the skyscraper. I look back down to ease the tension the sunlight puts on my eyes.

We walk through a crowd of commuters to the building's entrance. One of the men opens the door and we enter. I begin to walk slower than the men escorting me to look around in admiration of the main floor of the building.

The building contains several small shops on the ground floor food court, and a system of elevators provides transport to any floor of the building. The walls and columns are colored like a metallic rose. Crowds of people walk throughout the ground floor without caring that five men in suits are escorting a teenager. I guess everyone here just blends into the crowd.

One of the men places his hand on the back of my neck and pushes me ahead at a faster pace. We walk toward the elevators in the middle of the ground floor. People stand in line between velvet ropes at the elevator where they must go through security. The men escort me past the line and into a private elevator.

We enter the shiny box, and the five men push me to the back. I place my hands on the metal bar connected to the glass. Squeezing the bar tight, a slight shock shoots up my wrist from the cold metal. I glare out at the building. The elevator shoots up, and I look down in dread. I have no idea what awaits me on whatever floor we are heading to, but I do know I can handle it. I think I can.

A bell rings and the elevator opens. I turn around, and a man grabs my arm, directing me out of the elevator. We walk down a long hallway with silver walls and dark blue carpeting. I count about half a dozen guards posted along the walls of the hall. My neck turns every second to take in my surroundings.

These men wear cargo pants and long sleeve shirts of different, dark colors. Their weapons are not concealed, but holstered on proud display for anyone on this floor.

The hallway leads to an office protected by tall glass doors with gold trimming and handles. We walk ahead, and I can see a man sitting at a desk inside the office with someone else.

I reach the door, and one of the guards opens it. I enter the room with two of the suited men. The rest hang back. The office is huge with the same gold trim as the outside hallway.

On the wall to my right, two katanas hang parallel to each other. The handles are wrapped red over a gold base. I can see several other weapons on that same wall, including medieval axes and a golden bow with a quiver of bronze arrows resting on a metal stand. In the corner, I notice a metal door with a keypad attached.

Several black shelves hang on the gray wall on my left. One shelf holds a black statue of a falcon. Another shelf displays a variety of African war masks. Further down, a very old rifle hangs adjacent to a manikin clothed in oriental armor. Despite their obvious age, these weapons are in pristine condition.

Standing at the tall glass doors, I look directly ahead at a large black and silver desk a few feet away from the glass wall of the building, which reveals an astounding view of the city skyline.

Behind the desk, a man wears a black suit, a white collared shirt with black buttons, a well-fitted vest buttoned over a black and gold tie with a gold tie clip, and an expensive-looking Rolex. The man has black hair with gray creeping in around his temples and no facial hair. His face looks stern, but I don't think he is angry. I try not to focus on his overarching brow. A woman wearing a black and gold dress sits on the corner of the man's desk holding his tie.

"That's all I need for today, Evelyn," he tells her.

The woman he called Evelyn stands up and walks toward me. She looks down at my feet, and her eyes work their way up to my face. She smiles at me and leaves the office. My face burns from the attention of someone so pretty looking at me. I walk ahead toward the man, already impressed by him. This guy seems really cool.

The man looks at me and speaks in some sort of African accent, the specific country of origin I have no way of telling. "Please take a seat."

Before I sit down, I blurt out the question, "How do you know about my powers?"

"Patrick, that is no way to start a conversation. You should introduce yourself first," he tells me.

I'm not exactly sure why this stranger thinks he can chastise me after basically abducting me.

"That seems unnecessary since you obviously already know my name," I say to him.

"I suppose so. It is a nice courtesy nonetheless."

"Who are you?" I ask as I sit down across from him in a leather chair.

"My name is Adam."

I wait for further explanation that doesn't come.

"How do you know about my abilities?" I ask again.

"It wasn't very difficult after the incident at the hospital. And I wasn't the only one who figured it out, either. You're lucky I got to you before certain individuals—whom I will continue to leave unnamed—tried to take advantage of you," Adam says.

"What do you want?" I ask.

"Let's talk about you, Patrick. What do *you* want?" Adam says. "I can tell you if you like."

"Oh really? Then tell me," I challenge.

"You just got these powers, and now you want to be a superhero. Problem is, you're unsure how. Stop me if I'm wrong so far," Adam says.

"Keep going," I tell him. A slight, mischievous smirk forms at the corner of his lips.

"You feel that you have a responsibility to use your powers. But you need a purpose...a mission...a crusade."

"Did you bring me here to show off your fortune telling skills?"

"I don't tell people's fortunes, I forge them." Adam catches my attention. He continues, "I want to help you. Let me give you a purpose. I want you to adopt my crusade."

"And what's your crusade?"

"I do what you want to do. You want to save people—I have a plan to do it on a much larger scale than you could have ever hoped to be apart of."

Adam pauses, leaving me hanging on what he will say next. He stands up and walks to the window, looking out over the city. He continues, "I'm going to save the human race," he pauses for a for a few seconds and continues, "and I want you to help me."

"How are you going to save the human race?"

"I need to know you're on board first, before I tell you everything," Adam says.

"I'm not ready to give an answer," I tell Adam.

"That's fine; in fact, I prefer that response," Adam says turning around to face me. "I don't have any use for a man who gets himself into a situation without being prepared."

Adam walks closer to me and leans on the corner of his desk, closest to where I sit. He looks me in the eye and says, "Tomorrow I will have my car pick you up at the same time and place it did today. If you don't want your abilities to be wasted, you'll get in it."

"Who says my powers will be wasted? I don't need you," I tell Adam.

Any trace of joy disappears from his face and Adam responds with utter sincerity, "Fine. Go ahead and hang a tablecloth around your neck and fly around like a boy pretending to be a man. Continue on your path, and you'll save maybe a dozen people at the high end. After a month of balancing being a superhero with school and sports, you'll be a fugitive. The government will hunt you down because history has proven time and time again that the established order never approves of a new wave of people trying to make a difference. And, when they get you, the courts will make a motion requesting you be denied your basic human rights granted by the constitution based on the grounds that you are not human. You're a superhuman now, Patrick, so the rules don't apply to you. And, when you're in a lab with scientists trying to extract the source of your abilities from your DNA, you'll wish you had taken my offer. Join me and your crusade won't end with a few useless, unimportant individuals continuing on with their lives unappreciative of the sacrifice you made for them. Join me, and you'll save everyone...and they will know the name of their savior."

Saturday

2:50 P.M.

"Patrick, where are you going?" my mother asks.

"I'm going to see some friends, mom," I say to her.

"Patrick, I want to talk to you."

"About what?" I ask. She pauses at the harsh tone in my voice.

"Your leg," she says with bewilderment. "It's a miracle that it's healed."

"There's no such thing as miracles, Mom."

"Then how do you explain your leg?"

"You wouldn't understand."

"Sure I would."

"Mom, I have to go now."

"Patrick, you're acting different. You nearly killed that boy Trey at school."

"Trey was being a piece of shit," I tell her.

"Watch your language, Patrick Knight!"

"Sorry," I respond gently.

"I just want to make sure you're okay"

"Well, I am." My temper starts to grow.

"Maybe you should stay home today. Your brother misses you. You two never play together anymore," she pleads.

"Mom, I need to go, Kevin can play by himself," I tell her. "We'll talk later."

I slam the door behind me, and it cracks in half. I stop walking at the sound, realizing I lost control of my strength. I'm just angry. I have a detention to serve at three o'clock, but I'm not going. I refuse to waste another hour at school while people need my help. That school has already taken too much of my time away from me. I can't keep waiting until I'm an adult to start living my life. I want to start living now.

3:00 P.M.

I arrive at the same street corner where Adam's limo picked me up yesterday. The limo is predictably on time, and it drives me back downtown. We don't go to Adam's office this time. Instead, we arrive at a designer clothing store called Forrester's. Two men escort me into the building in the middle of Chicago's Loop. I look ahead and see Adam walking the aisles, wearing a black pea coat. I walk over to him, and see him beginning to pick out some clothes. He hands me a stack of dark pants and shirts and says,

"Here, these should fit you."

"What are these?" I ask.

"A superhero needs a costume right?" Adam says.

"I guess, but they usually wear something a little more colorful. These clothes are all black," I say.

"You need to be tactical. You're strong, but you're not invincible, so you need to be stealthy—learn to work in the shadows. These should help you blend in tonight," Adam says.

"Tonight?"

"That's right. There's no time like the present."

"What are we doing?" I ask.

"I had another speech prepared for you about stepping up to become a hero, but I thought showing you what I do would be best. Tonight we have a mission," Adam tells me.

"What's the mission?" I ask.

"You'll find out there. Meet me at the Sears Tower at 11:00."

"You mean the Willis Tower?"

"Call it whatever you like. I'll expect to see you there." He pauses and turns his head back to the racks of clothing. "Unless you're not ready to be a hero."

"Of course I am," I say with haste. "But, I need to have some idea of what we're doing though."

"No one will get hurt. Don't worry," he goes on. "Will you be there?" he faces the aisle but I notice him looking at my direction from the corner of his eye.

"You can count on it," I say.

"Good," Adam says. As an afterthought he adds, "And practice flying before then."

Adam leaves the clothing store with his security guards. I go into the store's fitting room and try on the clothes Adam purchased for me. He got me a pair of black cargo pants along with a long sleeved black shirt, a black leather jacket, a fitted black fabric jacket with a hood, black leather gloves, and a black balaclava mask with a slit cut to reveal the eyes like a ninja mask. He also left a pair of black boots at the dressing room.

I try on the clothes and feel powerful, like Adam. I stuff the mask in the pocket of my leather jacket and seal it in with the zipper. I wear the leather jacket over the durable, fabric jacket to combat the fierce Chicago winter. It gets so much colder near the lake.

I exit the store and pull the hood over my head. I look up and then around me on ground level as people pass by. I walk down the street, making a turn down the first alley I come across. I walk down slowly, keeping an eye out for other people. I start running. I race forward pushing myself up into the air on my fifth step.

I launch into the air, pushing my own limits. After several minutes of taking in the fresh air high above the ground, I approach the top of the building. I stretch my hands out and grip the edge of the roof. I pull myself up and roll out onto the gravel ground on the top of the skyscraper. I look out from this view and smile. Nothing compares to standing on the top of a skyscraper, alone, with no fear of death.

I keep running. I race to the end of the roof and take a risk. I leap off the building through a cloud. I immediately shut my eyes and soon find myself beyond the cloud. I open my eyes, tumbling to the ground a thousand feet down below. I wipe the perspiration coating my face from the cloud and push myself ahead.

I stay high on the roofs of buildings and circle between them to avoid being seen. I feel a sense of pride as flying gets easier.

The layers of clothing keep me warm at this altitude. I take deep breaths as gusts of wind from the lake pass by. When I fly, time seems to stop. It offers me a sense of peace as I hover over the people I've sworn to protect.

I feel my phone vibrating in my pocket, and as the phone calls get more frequent, I turn the device off. I'm tired of always worrying about what time it is and how much longer I have left in the day. I have a lot of time before the mission tonight. I've never felt such an immense sense of freedom before. Seeing the city like this...It makes me feel like I'm capable of great things.

The vibrant mango sun gleams with fading intensity between the buildings I pass between. I fly along a pack of birds soaring toward the river. I smile and soak in the knowledge that no one has ever experienced this. I laugh as I fly. It's a wonderful experience to laugh out of joy—not to impress others, but to simply express delight.

I watch the sky as it turns from a light, baby blue to indigo, then purple, and finally to a flushed black. The light in the sky becomes dimmer, but the city almost makes up for it with every street and office light that teems with a variety of radiant colors illuminating from the antennas and light posts at the peaks of buildings.

I sit down at the edge of an empty patio rooftop. I put the gloves in my pocket and feel the marble corner of the building. I shake off some of the dust. I grip the edge and move my upper body forward. I close my eyes out of fear and realize that's not an emotion that should control me. I open and look down.

I let go of my grip on the building. My feet dangle but haven't fallen yet. With a tiny thrust of force, I slide down the wall—just slightly. I keep a hand on the edge for balance, but I merely float there. I look down at all those people. They look so tiny from up here.

It's incredible how I used to spend all my time in constant worry. I'd be at home hustling to finish my homework so I could go to bed at a reasonable time. My life was work, work, work, and then more work. That was this week, too! Every time I was up late alone, this place was right here waiting for me. It's so quiet up here compared to the street-level commotion that comes from living in an urban metropolis.

I look up at the moon. As I stare at the moon, I realize that it's almost time. I'm excited.

Chapter 4

Saturday

11:00 P.M.

I stand at the Sears tower waiting for Adam. I keep my right hand in my pocket, and my left hand hangs down at my side holding the mask. The streets are significantly less populated at night.

My stomach starts churning. I have no idea what I'm about to get myself into. I want to impress Adam, but he might be expecting too much from me.

When Adam arrives, he makes a very noticeable entrance. Three black, armored trucks drive up to the side of the building, and Adam exits the vehicle with nearly a dozen armed men covered in body armor.

I take a breath, trying not to be phased by the dangerous weapons. Guns always look cool on TV and in video games, but now I realize how dangerous they can be. I've never been so close to a real gun, let alone a dozen automatic assault rifles. I can fly, but I'm not bullet proof. If Adam gave the order, I'd be at the whim of a firing squad.

A gun will shoot anyone without prejudice, but it's up to the person wielding the weapon to determine whether or not someone's life will continue. These men don't look like the most merciful individuals.

Adam approaches wearing black cargo-pants, an unzipped coarse black and charcoal coat, and black tactical gloves. His team takes position behind him at the fleet of cars they drove up in.

"You said no one would get killed," I say to Adam gesturing towards the armed men behind him.

"No one will...if you do your job," Adam says. "Get in the car. I'll explain what we're doing on the way there."

11:10 P.M.

I sit with Adam in the back seat of one of his trucks. We're joined by several of his other men. We drive through the city for about ten minutes. I don't take my eyes off their weapons once.

The vehicle pulls over in an alley beside a skyscraper I've never been to before. Adam removes his coat and sets it down on his seat. He exits the truck, and I follow him. We stand next to the building. I take a deep breath and look up.

"Fly us up to the roof."

"All of us?" I ask.

"Just us, Pat. We talked about stealth earlier. In order for that to work, we need to keep the team small, so it's just going to be you and me up there. Now, bring us up."

I grab onto his collar and then grab his left arm. I look up and focus. We start to elevate. I use all of my energy to keep steady to impress Adam, but it's difficult—if there's such a thing as flying muscles, mine still feel undeveloped.

As we coast up the building I ask Adam, "If it's just going to be us than why did you bring your army?"

"My men will remain at the base of the building and prepare to infiltrate it on my order, should anything go wrong. Let's hope we won't need them."

I look up and breathe in. I exhale and watch the moisture of the air molecules freeze in front of me. Carrying Adam through the air, I realize that he exhibits no signs of awe or even fear of the heights I carry him to. The man seems perpetually afflicted with a sense of melancholy and intense motivation.

I can start to feel the toll flying takes on my body without a break. It's gotten easier but it takes so long to soar to the top of a skyscraper that I start to feel dizzy.

Adam and I reach a patio near the top of the building, and I set us down on a brick path. As soon as I set him down, I turn around and start panting. Out of breath, I try not to throw up. I look around at the empty rooftop. Adam walks down the brick path to a door, which blocks the stairwell that gives access to the rest of the building. As we walk to the door, I say to Adam, "The door is probably locked. Do you have a key?"

"No," Adam responds.

"Oh...did you want me to kick it down or something?" I ask.

71

"No, I've got this one Pat."

Adam pulls out a pistol that was covered by his sweater. He reaches into his pocket and pulls out a thin, metal rod. Adam screws what I assume to be a silencer to the barrel of the gun. Adam aims the gun and shoots off the hinges. I look around nervously listening to the sound of bullet shells hitting the ground.

Adam walks forward and kicks down the door with his right foot as naturally as if it were another step. The door breaks off and slams on the tile floor. Adam walks over the door, and I follow him into the stairwell. The space is tight and very confined. We walk down the first flight of worn, lead-colored stairs.

Adam walks casually with the pistol at his side and says to me, "You're going to want to put your mask on now."

I nod and pull the mask over my head. I reach around the back of my head the tug the hood over the mask. Now dressed completely in black, Adam and I walk down two more flights of stairs when two security guards standing on the platform below spot us.

"Take them down," Adam orders me.

The guards each wear identical, short-sleeved, eggshell shirts with mustard security patches and black pants. A heavy belt secures their pants, and holsters a Taser.

I rush down a few steps and kick out with my right leg. I snap the leg forward and knock one of the guards down the stairs and into a wall. My immediate natural response is to apologize, but I stop myself.

The other guard winds up a left hook to my face. I freeze, still staring at the guard I kicked unconscious. The standing guard's arm bashes into my jaw, and I hunch over to my left grabbing the railing for support. I can't feel the cold metal with my black tactical gloves.

I shake my head and grab the side of my face that was hit. I've only been punched a few times in my life, but I expected it not to hurt as much this time because of my powers. Like Adam said earlier—I'm not invincible.

Adam leaps down the stairs with a shout. He strikes the guard along the carotid artery in his neck with an open hand. The guard flares out his teeth and clenches his jaw. Adam kicks the guard in his back leg, buckling his knee forward. The guard naturally responds by lowering his head, and Adam drives an elbow down into the guard's temple.

The guard tumbles down the stairs and falls on top of his partner. The two of them look like they're sleeping. Adam places his hand on my shoulder.

"Shake it off, you're doing great."

"Adam, you told me no one would get hurt. What was—" I respond, quickly interrupted.

"A necessary action for lives to be saved," he interjects. "You'll understand soon, just follow me."

I do as he says. We walk down one more flight of stairs and enter a door leading to a floor of offices filled with cubicles. Adam and I take cover behind a wall. He peers over our cover and prepares to move ahead.

I close my eyes and breathe deeply, taking in the surroundings. I stop using my eyesight and fall back on my echolocation. Walking the hallway beyond the wall, two more security guards patrol the office area. I open my eyes and see Adam stand. I grab his collar and hold him back.

"Adam, there are two guards in front of us."

"How do you know?" Adam asks.

"Echolocation," I tell him, pressing my fingers against my head.

"The things I could do with your abilities…Can you take one of them?" Adam asks.

"Definitely," I tell him.

Adam and I turn the corner and rush the guards. I run to the left and throw an aggressive punch at the guard's head. On Adam's order it becomes easier to start a fight with a stranger.

He ducks my punch and swings a kick at me. I grab his leg mid-strike and throw him through a cubicle, using his own force for leverage. I turn around and see Adam standing over the other unconscious guard. I use my echolocation on the patrolman Adam disabled. I notice the man has several broken ribs and his collarbone is completely fractured.

I give Adam some credit for being able to subdue the guard without killing him, but he certainly left a mark. Adam nods at me, and we begin to head down another hallway.

Adam walks in confident strides that I try to match. We walk down as far as the hallway extends and open a door to one of the offices. Adam takes out his pistol. He aims the gun at the hinges of the door and shoots them off, just like on the roof. The door falls, and I look around in fear that someone heard the loud cracking sound. Once I decide the coast is clear, I follow Adam into the room.

A chrome platform rests in the center of the room with a cubed piece of glass resting on top of it like a display case in a museum. The glass has a computer chip enclosed inside. Adam walks to the computer chip and places his left hand against the glass. He stares at the computer chip with great desire and tells me,

"I need you to break the glass."

"That's it?" I ask.

"The explosion large enough to shatter the glass would also destroy the chip. This is why I needed you here. I need a controlled force to extract the chip."

I walk up to the case and look around. I breathe in through my nose and out of my mouth. As I exhale, I wind up and slam my right fist into the glass. The glass shatters and falls to the floor and over the platform around the chip. I pick it up with my left hand and extend the chip to Adam. He takes it and puts the chip in his pocket.

I bring my left arm pack to my body and hold the hand I used to smash the glass. My right arm pulses and the hand feels wet wrapped in my glove. I start to peel off my glove and see blood smearing against my skin. I tuck the glove back over and keep it elevated near my body. The mask and hood help me hide the pain.

Suddenly, an alarm begins ringing. The burst of sound starts to resonate.

"Pat, make an exit through that wall," Adam says.

"What?" I ask in astonishment.

"We can't leave the same way we came in. This place is going to be flooded with security in a few seconds so *make us an exit*," Adam orders.

I crouch down and pick up the door Adam knocked down earlier. I throw the hollow, wooden door through the silver wall, creating a hole big enough for us to leave through. The door tumbles down the side of the skyscraper and shatters against the empty sidewalk below.

I grab Adam and jump through the crater, first staring out at the Chicago skyline, and then peering down at the ground down below. I feel a shock rush from my toes to my forehead as gravity brings us down. I use my abilities to slow the force down enough for us to survive the fall.

12:00 A.M.

We make our getaway riding off in one of his trucks. Adam holds onto the chip like he has his heart in his hand. I look at the chip and then up at Adam and ask, "Adam, why did we steal that chip?"

"This is an advanced navigational chip developed by Gamboa Industries. This was going to be shipped off to the nearest military base tomorrow night. This chip would have been used on a new drone that would have killed hundreds if not thousands of people. Now, those people get a second chance. What you just did saved a lot of people. This is what I do, Patrick. Tell me, do you want to keep saving lives?" Adam says.

"Definitely."

Sunday
9:20 P.M.

"And you took down three security guards?" Daniel asks me.

"It was just two," I say to Daniel, who looks disappointed. "Actually, on second thought, I think it was four."

"You're such a badass," Daniel says, looking at his feet and then ahead.

Dan and I continue walking down the city streets, a slight mist pouring down from the clouds. The rain is more refreshing than annoying. We had some fast food for dinner, and now we're just walking around the loop.

"What time do your mom and dad want us back at your place?" I ask

"My mom wants us home by ten. My dad could care less," Daniel answers. "He doesn't even come home most nights."

"Does he work a night shift at the hospital?"

"He doesn't work at a hospital anymore," Daniel tells me.

"Oh really? What happened?" I enquire.

"He got this new job a few months ago—this private military group."

"What's he doing?"

"He's working on this gene therapy stuff. It's good work and I'm proud of him and all...I just never see him. And when he is around, he's fighting with my mom."

"That sucks man," I tell him. "That really does."

"Holy crap!" Daniel shouts, "I think someone's getting mugged in that alley!"

"What?"

Dan and I stop in our tracks and look down the alley on our right. The darkness prevents us from making out any figures but we can easily hear a struggle accompanied by shrieks for help.

I walk ahead into the dark shadowy gap between buildings and zip up my leather jacket. I take the mask out of my pocket and tug it over my head. I walk down the alley and stomp over a pool of mud. The splash from the muddy water reveals my presence to the two muggers as I adjust my hood over the mask on my head.

I see a man wearing a dirty, burnt cinnamon jacket hitting a woman, pinning her up against a brick wall. His accomplice wears a bone colored hoody and kicks a man on the ground. The man screams in pain and the woman shrieks in fear. Thunder strikes in the distance. It gives way to a downpour of rain.

I approach the thug wearing the burnt cinnamon jacket and clench my hands into fists after adjusting my gloves. I grab his long, dirty blonde hair with both of my hands and squeeze his skull as I slam his head into the brick wall. I let go of the criminal and he drops to the ground, with scarlet blood oozing from a crack I left at the top of his head. The blood pours from the gash in his face and down his neck, leaving a stream of crimson over his spider tattoo.

The man and woman run off immediately. I look down at the criminal with long hair and hear him crying out in pain. I crouch down next to him and begin to hit him in the back of the head. My fist bashes into the back of his skull. It stings, but I don't let the pain stop me from letting my anger loose. I can start to see his blood on my knuckles and I stop. I can sense his heart still beating. He's alive, but certainly not conscious.

The man in the bone colored hoody tries to punch me with a wild, right hook as I crouch down over his friend. I turn into him, extending out my left arm to block the hand and sink my hands into his hoody. I clench the fabric, his friends blood wiping off onto it. I swing his entire body into a wall. His head jolts back, colliding with the brick. I keep ahold of the criminal and do the same on the opposite wall. Fragments of the brick crumble to the ground as the man lets out a shriek.

I drop the man down on his feet and slam him into the side of the building. I hold his neck in my left hand and punch him in his teeth with my right fist. I hear a crack, not knowing if the sound originates from my knuckles or his mouth, but I continue, squeezing his throat tightly.

I strike him a second time and his eye turns black and blue as a spurt of blood squeezes out. I prepare to hit him again when someone grabs my arm and holds me back. The voice says,

"If you hit him again you'll kill him!" I let go of the mugger, turn around, and punch the person holding my hand back. Then I realize Daniel had grabbed my arm. He shouldn't have tried to stop me. I watch as my friend falls to the ground.

I return to hitting the mugger. I punch him in the chest a few more times, listening to his chest cavity crack as blood begins building up in his mouth. Someone grabs my arm again. I try to fight it but my arm feels immobilized. If it's Dan trying to stop me again, I'll kill him.

I turn around and look at the person trying to stop me from hurting the criminal. It's not Dan. Instead, I see someone I've never met before.

The man holding my arm back this time wears a metallic black armored suit with silver plates attached to the chest, arms, and legs. A ruby red glow glimmers from his silver visor on his smooth black helmet. The same bright red color glows from within the armor and expels from the seams and cracks in the suit. I look back at my own ruby-outlined reflection in his suit. The rain pours over his suit like a waxed car. The water droplets gleam red like the energy source that powers the suit.

The man's armor looks alien. I stare directly ahead into his visor, studying the technology. I shiver with the cold droplets of rain tapping on my head, the water seeping through the hood into my mask. The man's sleek armor seems as easy to move in as my clothing. I look at his shoulder and find that he has a cape attached to the armor. The cape itself looks like obsidian, but it doesn't appear to be made of fabric. It looks like a thin metal, with a silver foil streaming within it.

I drop the mugger and throw a left hook at the armored man. He ducks and pivots around me. I hear cars rush past out on the street and the rain pouring against the sides of the buildings and pooling up on the ground.

I turn around to face him and watch as he touches his neck with his middle and index fingers. The spot he touches glows like a cherry over the jet-black armor. After he presses against the area on his neck, his cape retracts into his neck plating on his backside, like a roll of measuring tape.

"I don't want to fight. I just want—" The man in the armor says calmly before I interrupt him.

I kick at the man with a right front kick. He steps to his left, dodging my foot. As I miss, my momentum carries my foot through the wall behind where he previously stood. I pull my foot, tearing out several bricks along with it. Light shines out from the interior of the building I just created a crater in.

I enter a fighting stance, bouncing back and forth like an amateur boxer. I dive forward and throw a left straight. My wild and uncontrolled punch tears another hole in the brick wall above where I kicked. My arm passes through the wall as if it weren't even there, tearing out several more bricks. I look back at the destruction I caused in disbelief. My bare fist created it.

My arm begins to ache as I tear it out of the wall. My next blow finally reaches the man in the armored suit who ducks down to the ground with great speed. As the armored man crouches, I kick him with my right foot. The man catches my leg and says, "Please, I just want to talk with you." He lets go of my foot.

A part of me wants to know what he has to say. Unfortunately, the part that doesn't care is too angry to listen to him. I attack him with a left straight punch. He ducks under it and slides behind me. I swivel my head to face him, and my body follows with a roundhouse kick. He blocks the kick with his right arm, striking at the side of the limb. I drop my leg to the ground, slamming it down into a pile of mud and debris. I regain my balance, acknowledging no visible dent in the armor on his blocking arm.

This guy must be getting tired—I know I am. I charge at him and, to my own surprise, land a hit. I grab his neck and lift him off the ground. I carry him through the air and run while trying to push him into a wall. As we get close to another section of the brick side of the building, the armored man presses two fingers against his thigh and disappears.

The armored man teleports away just as my hand hits the wall. A shock rushes up my wrist. I hold my striking hand in the other arm. I look around trying to locate the man who attacked me. I hear his voice and look up to see him standing high above me on a fire escape.

"I don't want to fight you, Patrick. I just want to talk," the man says.

"Then talk," I tell him, wiping the rain drops from my eyes.

The armored man jumps down from the fire escape, with his cape drawn out acting as a parachute.

"Who are you?" I ask.

"I am The Chimaera—The Last Time Agent," the armored man tells me.

"What do you want?"

"I've come here to help you," The Chimaera tell me.

"I don't need your help," I say.

"Trust me, Pat, you do," he tells me, retracing the cape once more.

"Even if I did need your help, what qualifies you to give it?"

"It is my mission to help people like you. I spend every second of my life trying to help people like you save the world. I seek out individuals who have discovered that they bare great skills and abilities. I can teach you—train you. I want you to live up to your potential."

"Why do you want to train me?"

NICHOLAS CHIMERA

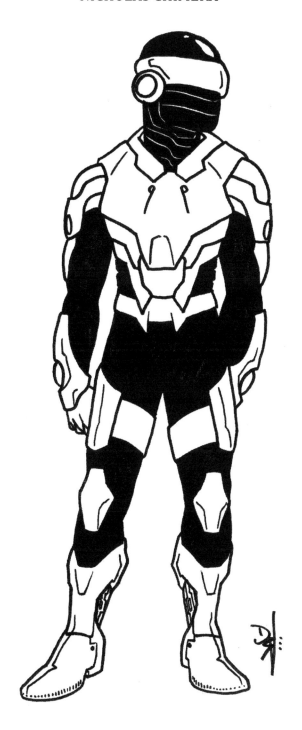

THE CRUSADER

"For me, this has already happened. I'm a time traveler. I have fought alongside you many times. You will become a great hero some day...a Crusader. I am just playing my role in setting history on the correct course."

"I don't need your help."

"But you don't deny that you need help. Right now, you think Adam is the only help you need. You think he understands what you are going through but believe me, he does not care about you."

"Adam wants to save the world," I say, moving past my initial surprise of hearing his name. We both start to circle each other.

"Adam doesn't want to save the world, he wants it to burn. And he doesn't care about you. He is only using you to move his plan along," The Chimaera tells me.

"How do you know about Adam?"

"You may think he is your ally, but one day soon he will become your greatest enemy."

"You're wrong."

"I've seen it happen."

"I'm done listening to you," I say, inching forward.

"I will stay away for now, but I want you to know that when Adam betrays you and when you think you have no more friends left, I will be there," The Chimaera says.

The Chimaera takes out a gold and blue pocket watch from a pocket in his armor. He opens the watch and presses against it. The Last Time Agent teleports away.

I let out a scream. I look around, pacing in anger. The two muggers lay nearly dead on the ground. And Daniel is still unconscious from my punch.

The Chimaera spoke like he was from the future. I'm not going to turn my back on Adam just because of what some armored man says about him in an alley. But what if I was too quick to put my trust in Adam?

Right now I need to help my friend. I walk over to Dan. I crouch down next to him and try to help him stand. He won't open his eyes, but I can see him breathing. I lean him up against the wall of the alley and sit on the ground next to him.

I close my eyes and let out a deep sigh. I take off my mask and gloves and set them on my lap. My right wrist pierces with pain, bending a little too much to the left. The skin is white and red. I wipe off the blood from my knuckles onto my jacket. I hold out my hands and let the rain clean off the rest.

These wounds hurt now, but at least I know they'll heal soon. No one will have to know what happened here in this alley.

I look over at Dan. His wounds won't heal the way mine will. He has a bruise on his right cheek, but the swelling should go down by the end of the week. I shouldn't have attacked him. I betrayed my friend.

It was my fault when we stopped hanging out sophomore year. And now, just when we start our friendship up again, I punch him in the face. I can't believe I did this to him.

Dan's eyes slowly open and he takes in a deep breath. He wipes away a tear from his eye, soon feeling the bruise in his skin. I lift him up onto his feet.

"Dan, I am so sorry."

"Let's go," Daniel says.

"Dan, please forgive me."

"I just want to go home."

I nod, and we step out of the alley, onto the street. We start walking back to his apartment in silence. I have no idea what to say. My phone starts buzzing in my pocket. I pull out the phone and answer a call from Adam. I clear my throat and speak.

"Hello?"

"Hello, Patrick. Are you up for another mission?" Adam asks.

"Definitely," I respond.

"A car will pick you up at the usual spot at five tomorrow.

Chapter 5

Monday

5:49

I didn't like talking to The Chimaera. I don't trust him, but, he created a suspicion of Adam in my mind. I've put my complete trust in someone I met a few days ago. But I've never felt so free in my life. I've been alone and I'm using my powers the way I think I should be using them. No one's telling me what to do every minute of my day like before. Adam's offering a sense of direction—I just need to decide if it's the right way.

If anything The Chimaera told me was true, then I need to be much more weary of Adam.

The guards open the doors to Adam's office and I walk in to see him sitting at his desk. Adam gestures me over. I walk to his desk, admiring his wall of weapons and armor again. I sit down in the chair across from him. Adam opens his mouth as if to speak but a familiar security guard enters the room and interrupts him.

"Sir, you have a call from the General," the guard says.

"Thank you," Adam responds. The security guard exits the room and Adam addresses me. "Patrick, would you mind waiting while I take this call?"

"Not at all," I tell him.

Adam rises from his chair and buttons his suit coat. He walks around the desk, patting my shoulder as he walks past me. I turn around and make sure he's left the room.

I breathe in, exhale, and tilt my head, while I attempt to sense Adam with my echolocation. I've recently practiced training my mind to place color to certain objects—nothing detailed, but enough to distinguish moving things. I remain sitting in my chair, following Adam with a mental picture.

I assumed one of Adam's guards would hand him a phone, but they didn't. Adam walks directly to the elevator. He gets in at the end of the hall, and after a few minutes exits on the seventh floor. He walks to the end of the floor below and into a room. By this point, the other people and offices in this building distract my mind and keep me unfocused.

If I'm going to keep an eye on Adam, I need to get closer to him. I hesitantly stand up from my chair and walk around the room, pretending to peruse his artifacts. I slowly make my way to a corner of the room beyond the view of the guards from the outside hallway.

I unlock the latch and open the window in the corner— just enough to slide out. I look down below at the cars honking and pedestrians walking the city streets. They're so focused on where they're going they never stop to look up.

I take a deep breath and climb out the window. For a second, fear takes over as gravity tugs me down to the earth below. I keep a calm head and use my energy to hold my body up. My falling speed slows down and I slide down the building toward the seventh floor. I lower myself slowly, brushing my hands against the wall as I hold myself up in the air. I subconsciously feel the need to remain connected to something when I fly, grazing along the side of the building.

I try to remember which part of the floor I last saw Adam. I focus in and search for his voice. I slide over to the edge of the building. I place my back up against the side of the building's metal wall and close my eyes. Thanks to my powers, I can both see and hear Adam through the blockade of matter.

Adam walks to a panel and clicks a button. Light molecules shine on his face. Adam starts to speak with his words directed to the screen on a massive computer shell.

"General Barringer. Thank you for checking in," Adam says, much clearer than the scratchy sounds from the computer's speaker.

"It is necessary to ensure that the plan is running smoothly," the mysterious voice from the computer says.

"Everything on my end is running perfect. I've taken on a protégé actually—someone with abilities."

"Like Indomitus?"

"Not to his degree of power, but yes. This kid can fly, he has incredible strength. Some echolocation, sonar sense too.

He's quite remarkable," Adam continues, "He assisted me with our last mission, to retrieve the navigation chip."

"Yes, we received the broken down schematic scans you sent. The Nomads are currently using it to update their missile guidance systems."

"Excellent. I've placed the devices in the key locations that we agreed upon. It's taken a few decades, but that part of the plan has been completed. They're scheduled to activate once the Nomads arrive."

"Good. The Nomads are scheduled to arrive in your system in two of your days. The invasion will commence soon after that," General Barringer continues, "Are there any other problems we need to address?"

"I have an issue regarding Indomitus," Adam goes on, "Will he be a problem with the plan?"

"Not at all. He's been on escort to Earth for over forty years now. He has over half a century to go too, assuming he doesn't kick the ship's engines into over drive. And he's too scared to do it. The last time he reached the ship's top speed...well, I found him a few billion light years from home."

"I know all about that. I just don't like being at the whim of someone else. If he decided he wanted to risk overdrive again, he could be here in time to stop the invasion and this would be over."

"That's never going to happen. And even if he suddenly decided to take that risk, the invasion would still succeed."

"How?" Adam asks.

"I am prepared to talk to him and explain our situation. I know that if I order him to stand down, he will."

"You think he will just abandon his species?" Adam asks.

"You did," General Barringer states. He pauses and then continues, "Trust me, he still wears the uniform I gave him. He will follow my orders."

"And what if he doesn't? You told me many years ago it would take God to kill him."

"Adam, this man fought for me. He went to war with an alien galaxy because he felt a moral obligation to defend free choice. I have his loyalty. He will not worry about his own people after the invasion. Everyone he loved is gone. He's not connected to them anymore."

"I know the feeling," Adam mutters.

"When this is all over, I get a planet flushed with tremendous recourses, ruled by a species fully indebted to the Alpha-Omega Galaxy. And you," Barringer adds, "You get what you've always wanted." Barringer assures.

"Good. Is that all?" Adam asks.

"It is. Good luck to you," General Barringer says.

Adam turns off the panel and begins to walk back upstairs. I quickly fly up the side of the building toward Adam's floor trying to make sense out of what I just heard. It sounds insane, but it sounds as though Adam is assisting some sort of an invasion of the Earth by a group of beings from another world that Adam and the general referred to as "the Nomads."

I climb up to the window in Adam's office and grab the opening. I pull myself up and fall onto the floor in his office. I quickly shut the window and race back to the chair across from his desk. I present myself like I haven't moved. Luckily, no one noticed my absence.

I can't believe what I've just heard. I lose control of my breathing and start sweating. My head bobs up and down and my legs shake. My elbows keep flailing out...I think I'm having a panic attack. I can't have a panic attack in Adam's office! I adjust my hair and straighten my shirt. I start coughing. Adam walks back into the room.

"I apologize. That was a very important call."

"I'm sure it was," I tell him, with a crack in my voice.

"So, would you like to know about our next mission?" Adam asks.

"Yes," I say slowly, "Yes I would."

"Tomorrow at seven-thirty there will be an illegal shipment of weapons coming into Navy Pier."

"You want to steal them?" I ask.

"Of course not. You're going to blow up the boat so no one has to die at the hands of those guns," Adam tells me.

"Blow up the boat? That action could hurt just as many people as the threat you're trying to stop."

"Your job will be to evacuate the boat's crew," Adam says, sounding annoyed. "Get them to safety and then blow up the vessel and sink the weapons."

Adam seems like he wants to help people, but his conversation with General Barringer certainly suggests otherwise. I'm still not sure if he's trustworthy or not. He could be lying to Barringer, or he could be lying to me. Either way there's something bigger at play here, and the world could be at stake.

"Sounds Good. I will meet you at the pier tomorrow then," Adam says.

"Sure," I respond with a nervous gulp, "Do you have any missions we can go on today?"

"There is always something to be done, but for right now I think you should go home. Maybe spend some time with your family."

"Spend time with them? They don't understand me."

"You're going to learn that very few people ever will. But Patrick, just because they don't know the real you doesn't mean they still can't be part of your life. Let them think they know who you are. Then, when you need it, you will have every advantage over them, and they will have nothing on you. I don't necessarily mean this as advice for dealing with your parents," Adam says with a grin, "but it's always good to make sure no one understands what's in your head. Do this and you will be truly unpredictable. And when you can't be predicted no one can stop you."

7:00 P.M.

Adam's driver drops me off a few blocks off from my house and I walk the rest of the way. I'm looking forward to my next mission tomorrow. I've been itching for a good fight lately.

I arrive at the house and go through the front door. I walk toward the living room and call out to see if anyone's home.

"Mom...Dad?" I hear no response. "Kevin?"

I hear the faint sounds of sniffling. I walk into the living room and see Kevin curled up in a ball on the couch, crying. I look at him and see that he has a black eye. I clench my fists and my head begins to shake with fury.

"Kevin, are Mom and Dad home?" I ask.

"No," Kevin says softly.

"Who did this to you, buddy?" I ask him.

"It was Bobby from school," Kevin tells me.

"Trey's little brother?"

"He's not little to me," Kevin says with gloom.

"You two were friends. You slept over at his house once. I remember walking you over there. Why did he hit you?"

"I don't know. He just changed. He started making fun of you. He called you a freak and I told him to stop. Then, he punched me," Kevin continues, still crying. "Please don't tell Mom or Dad. I don't want Bobby to get in trouble."

"I won't tell Mom or Dad, but believe me. Bobby is in big trouble."

I run upstairs and grab my leather jacket. I throw it on and zip it up. I put on my tactical gloves as I race down the stairs.

Kevin asks me, "Patrick, where are you going?"

"I won't be gone long, Kevin."

I run out the door and put on my mask, violently pulling it down over my face. I sprint down the street towards Bobby's house, my arms flailing as my body violently shifts weight from one side to the next. I'll kill Trey for making his little twerp of a brother beat mine up.

7:10 P.M.

Bobby's house is white and gray with a balcony on the second floor. I arrive at the house and kick down the front door. I walk in over the door and punch my left palm with my right fist. I angrily yank my hood up over the mask. I immediately see Bobby and Trey standing by the spiral staircase that leads to the second floor.

"Bobby, run to your room!" Trey yells.

Bobby runs up the stairs. Trey grabs a baseball bat from the corner and blocks the stairs. I hear Bobby's footsteps slam into the wooden steps as he races to the second floor. I walk to the stairs feeling pure rage. I want to murder that kid for hurting my brother and I'll kill anyone that gets in my way.

"Get out of my house, punk!" Trey yells.

"Ready for round two, scumbag!" I roar.

Trey looks puzzled but readies the baseball bat. I reach the stairs and Trey swings the bat at me. I grab the wooden piece of baseball equipment with my left hand and tear it out of his hand. I crack it over my right knee and hold two pieces of sharp wood in each hand. I hit Trey over the head with the piece of the bat in my left hand, shattering the wood into several more chunks. They clatter as they hit the ground. Trey falls to the ground too, but quickly tries to lift himself up. I smile.

Trey stands and punches me in the gut. It hurts, but my adrenaline fuels my power and I scream at him, "Hit me again! Do it!"

Trey repeatedly strikes at my chest and stomach. I breathe heavily and shake off his attempts to stop me.

I slap him with the back of my hand and he falls back to the stairs. He holds onto the railing, and I stab the other end of the sharpened baseball bat through his leg. Trey squeezes the railing as the tendons in his arms and neck bulge and throb under his skin. Trey screams and starts crying. I walk over him, leaving the end of the baseball bat sticking out of his thigh.

"Useless," I remark as I make my way up the stairs slowly.

I feel a rush of adrenaline from the fight with Trey—but now I want his brother. I turn right at the top of the spiral staircase and find Bobby's room. I twist the handle to the door. It won't turn. I smile again, but my mask covers the expression.

I push the door in and it flies across the room. As I enter, I see Bobby on the floor in the corner of the room with his knees clenched into his chest. He scratches his nails along the fabric of his pants. He shuts his eyes, tucking his head between his knees, terrified of the monster at his door.

His mother runs into the room behind me. I could sense her coming with my echolocation, so as she runs up to me, she fails to catch me off guard. Bobby's mother grabs my face and tries to tear off the mask. I turn around and grab her shoulders. I throw her to the ground and she slides across the hardwood floor to her son. She looks up to him and holds up her hands.

"Please, don't hurt my baby," she pleads.

I walk to the kid and stand over him. I clench my hands together. The mother stands up and punches me in the chest repeatedly. She's not powerful enough to stop me, and no one else is around to save them. No one can stop me.

The mother slaps me across the face and her wedding ring cuts my cheek. I shove her in the chest, pushing her into the wall. She falls down, unconscious. Bobby calls out to his mother.

I walk next to Bobby and stand over him. He just stood there as he watched me nearly kill his mother. I can sense her heart still beating, but he must think she's dead. I grab him and hold him up in the air. Bobby begins to cry.

The sound of his sobbing brings me back to myself and I realize what I've done. I harmed a mother protecting her sons and an older brother looking out for his younger sibling—a situation that's far too familiar.

What did I think I was going to do to this kid? What happened to me? How could I let my anger get control of me like this? My powers did this to me. The power I wield has corrupted my conscience and turned me into a monster. I hate what I've become.

I set Bobby down on his feet. The boy runs out of his room and down the stairs to Trey, who fell unconscious from the shock and now lays stretched out on the floor. I fall to my knees, tears soaking through my mask. I tear it off and hold it in both of my hands. I stare at the mask as my tears drip onto it, mixing with Trey's blood.

My grammar school principal used to say, "You're true self is the person you are when you're alone. You are what you do when you think no one is watching." I've been left alone this past week, and I took my powers and hurt others.

I thought I was a good person. I got good grades in school and I never hurt anybody. Then, I got these powers and I changed. Anyone could be as angry as I am now. But very few people actually have the means I do to let their anger cause this much damage.

I close my eyes and think back to those criminals in the alley downtown. They could be dead for all I know—all that blood because of what I did to them. And now, Trey may never walk again.

I thought these powers were a gift given to me for protecting others. I'm supposed to be God's Crusader, but now I feel like the barer of a curse plagued upon me by the devil, forcing me to do evil unto others and spread chaos throughout the Earth. I tried to be a hero, but I only caused more suffering. I used heroism as a front for hurting people, and in so doing I became a villain.

I stand up, and walk down the stairs past Bobby and his brother. The boy looks at me. I see fear and hatred in his eyes. The anger I felt became an infection that has now caught ahold of this poor child. I stole this boy's innocence and I can never change that.

All I can do now is fly away. I fly home and lock myself away in my room. I take off my jacket, gloves, and mask, and throw them to the ground. Starting to cry again, I climb into bed and pull my blanket tight around me. I can't believe what I've done.

"What am I?" I ask myself. "Who am I?"

Why can't I be a good person? Why did I let my rage control me? Why did I let these powers change me?

I look over at my desk. I see three marble shaped objects, which illuminate with a bright, amethyst glow. I climb out of bed and walk over to them. The tiny spheres rest on a note, taped to several manila file folders.

"When you need help and think there is no one left to trust, throw one of these and I will be there. – The Chimaera"

I pick up the orbs and examine them, holding them up to the light in my room and seeing the purple glow from the cracks in the metal. I set the orbs down gently and swipe the note aside. I pick up the manila folders and open them up. I begin reading through the documents The Last Time Agent left me.

THE CRUSADER

Isabelle Thompson

Supervising engineer on *NAVIGATO* Project

May 19th, 1969

One day away from NAVIGATO Project Launch

I met with a colleague I worked with on Gemini at a coffee shop around 1 AM. He went out on a limb to tell me everything he did, and to insure his own personal safety, I've decided to leave his name out of my written accounts. My colleague works in the flight control division. I was lucky that his guilt outweighed the fear he felt as a result of spilling government secrets.

He informed me that after the *NAVIGATO* launch, the Air Force fully intends to send up the ship again and fire off a dozen nuclear missiles in areas controlled by the Soviet Union. A full-scale nuclear conflict will certainly result, and though the U.S. will likely win with the *NAVIGATO* on its side, a nuclear war between the two superpowers will either destroy the Earth itself or create devastating long-term consequences.

I went straight to Richard's apartment after hearing this. Richard was just as surprised as I was. We stayed up until 3 AM discussing our options. Despite being an active member of the United States Military, even he realized that nuclear war with Russia is the last thing the world needs. We realized the suspicion and possible incarceration we might bring on if we both dropped out of the project the day before launch. Our solution was to finish the *NAVIGATO* mission and see if Richard could reach out to higher ranking U.S. Generals to put a stop to this.

I was exhausted, but I couldn't sleep— I was too scared. Richard kept a pistol on him and gave the weapon to me. He told me to hold onto it until he came back from the launch. I have no idea what's going to happen tomorrow. I don't know if Richard and I can stop this.

THE CRUSADER

NICHOLAS CHIMERA

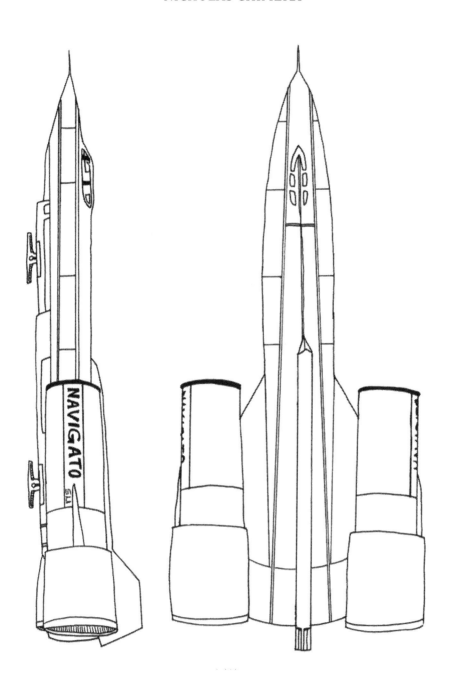

THE CRUSADER

Isabelle Thompson
Supervising engineer on *NAVIGATO* Project
Cape Canaveral Air Force Station, Florida
May 20th, 1969
NAVIGATO Project Launch Day

This is my final entry describing the events of the *NAVIGATO* mission. I am currently writing this from a sealed door in the on-site launch bunker. I can hear them trying to break through, so in what I assume are my final moments I express only the truth.

Thirty minutes before launch, my Gemini contact informed me that Colonel John Wilkins was ordered to take control of the helm and fire off nuclear missiles from space. I spent the next half hour pacing in my office with no idea what to do. Richard was up in the ship a few miles away and I felt entirely alone.

I couldn't let countless people die because of the ship I designed. Immediately after launch, I decided to resort to drastic measures. I entered the launch room and took out the gun Richard gave me. No one expected me to be a security threat and I got out of the weapons search earlier.

I took one of the communication officers hostage. I held the gun to his head and took control of his communication console. I called in to the *NAVIGATO* and told Richard that Wilkins had orders to fire a dozen nukes onto the surface of the planet. I told him I only had one option left and it was to destroy the beast I created by sacrificing the person I love most in the world.

Some of the guards thought I was bluffing and tried to move on me. I had to shoot one in the leg, as I quickly moved over to the remote piloting console. I entered engine input instructions and sent them up to the *NAVIGATO* in orbit with approval on my end. The pilot just had to input the flight path. I assume Richard had to fight Wilkins on it. The struggle itself may have torn up their flight suits. And if that didn't kill them, the flight path I entered would.

We knew from the beginning how dangerous the power source was. The theoretical physicists on my team told me that at maximum power, without any time for cool-down, transitioning past the speed of light into overdrive without any time for engines to adjust could tear a hole in space. That's why we launched the aircraft like a rocket first, so it wouldn't tear the planet apart. They kept the whole thing classified so no one would have to know if we failed.

I know Richard was able to input the orders from above because the launch site immediately lost contact with the *NAVIGATO*. When I knew the ship was gone, I broke down in tears. Mr. Akashi ran at me, without any regard for the hostage's life. I had no intention to kill anyone. Anyone except for

Richard Wilde and John Wilkins. Out of fear, I shot Akashi in the stomach. I dropped the gun sobbing. I ran out the nearest door and locked myself into the adjacent room.

Here I am. I've killed three people, destroyed billions of dollars of equipment, and lost the only person I love. What have I done? I may have saved many more lives than the three I've taken, but I lost my soul doing it. I should have died up there with Richard.

The guards are about to get through the door. I may wind up in prison for the rest of my life. They may kill me when they get through the door. I don't care what happens to me. My life is over now. I've atoned for the sin I committed when I built that ship. But can anyone ever atone for letting down the people they love?

THE CRUSADER

Jack Hayes
USAF Security Force Internal Affairs
Cape Canaveral Air Force Station, Florida
May 22nd, 1969

Whatever events transpired here, at Cape Canaveral Air Force Base two days ago never should have happened. Ms. Isabelle Thompson was found in the middle of the hallway at an undisclosed launch site with three bullets in her back.

Victim appears to have been chased and shot from ten feet away. I found the bullet casing in the middle of a pile of blood. The murderer seems to have been wounded when he or she killed Ms. Thompson.

Despite my best efforts to find one, it appears as though no official personnel list exists for this project; therefore, I have no clear-cut suspect. Following some preliminary interviews with her family members, it appears that Ms. Thompson was seeing an Air Force Pilot—Lieutenant Colonel

Richard Wilde. Richard Wilde is unaccounted for and remains the only potential suspect, though my gut says otherwise.

What bothers me most about this case is despite whether or not I could find whomever is responsible, several air force generals have urged me to discontinue my investigation. Ms. Thompson's Murder, and Lieutenant Colonel Richard Wilde's disappearance will remain a mystery indefinitely.

Chapter 6

Wednesday

1:10 A.M.

I stand on Navy Pier waiting for Adam. I can't stop thinking about Monday night and how I lost control. I need to make some major changes in my life. The path I'm on now will not take me anywhere I want to go. I've come to think of Adam as a father. That's what makes it so hard to decide where to go next.

First and foremost, I need to figure out what's going on with Adam. From his conversation with General Barringer, it sounds like he wants to destroy the human race. I'm not sure what I should—or even can—do about it. I'm not willing to declare war against Adam because of one out-of-context conversation. However, it might be the only way to stop him if he truly wants to destroy the Earth rather than protect it.

I don't want to believe Adam is evil. Since I first met him, I thought he was just like me. If Adam wants to kill that many people, then I share in his potential for destruction. I don't want that.

Assuming Adam needs to be stopped, I would need help to do it. I'm not sure if I can trust The Chimaera, but he might be the only person I know who can help me fight Adam. The problem is I can't stop myself from wondering if he is conspiring with Adam, too. I can't trust anyone.

I leave my leather jacket unzipped, displaying my long sleeved white shirt underneath. I hold onto my mask and gloves in my coat pocket. I stand watching over the water. I've hurt so many people. That's not what makes me a hero. And it's certainly not my powers either. The only time I've ever felt like a hero was at the hospital fire—and even then, I wasn't able to save everyone. I cannot continue on this path. I pull out my mask from my pocket and throw it into the water in a spurt of anger and regret.

Adam pulls up with his fleet of trucks and the small army of private security. Adam wears all black as usual. I notice that all of his soldiers wear heavy body armor, yet Adam walks as confident as the men who think they're bulletproof.

Adam hands me a large bomb. I hold onto three sticks of honey colored powder wrapped in plastic rectangles with several wires and a timer attached.

I hold it in my hands and he instructs, "Fly to the ship, plant the bomb, and set the timer. If you feel the need to save the crew, there are four of them on board. I'd look out for security though. We think there are six to eight men standing guard on the ship."

"I shouldn't be too long."

"We'll be waiting here," Adam says. "You need to move quickly."

I bend my legs and prepare to jump. I close my eyes and feel the air around me. I take off, flying toward the ship, pushing myself over the lake. I lower myself to the water and let my right hand hang down. I pass my fingers through the water in the lake a few feet beneath me. The chilled water cools the blisters on my knuckles. The jet-black sky reflects off the lake, but the water that surges up from contact with my hand is transparent.

I reach the boat and begin to hover over the vessel. I scan over the ship and take a count of the people on board. Adam's right—there are four crewmembers, but only five guards. I'm lucky that all the crewmembers are in the same place: on the bridge of the ship.

I fly to the bridge, and walk in. I yell, "Everyone, evacuate the ship, now!"

The bridge crew remains silent at first, but they scramble as I slam my hand through a wall. The crewmen run out to an emergency inflated raft, and take off away from the ship. The coast guard will pick them up after they hear the explosion. Now, I have to deal with the security.

I exit the bridge and climb to the top deck. I find a view where I can overlook the entire cargo vessel. I close my eyes and let my senses work. I find two guards standing near each other around a nearby grouping of shipping crates. If I make some noise, they will all gather in one place. I'd be able to take them out faster that way but doing so would be more difficult as I would lose the element of surprise.

I run off the deck and leap ahead. I fall to a lower level of the ship near an empty, squared off area between containers. I land on top of one of the guards, taking him out of the fight. Standing up from the guard's body, another guard to my right with gray hair takes out a pistol from his holster and aims it at my head. I grab the barrel of the gun with my right hand, and his arm with my left. I spin him to the right and throw him at a red cargo container scraped enough to show its original silver color.

I turn my back to the guard with gray hair, as he slams into the crate. I turn around quickly. I assumed that throwing the guard into a metal shipping container would knock him out, but the man proves me wrong. He grabs me in a chokehold. He wraps his arm around my neck and pulls me down, squeezing my head and jerking it around.

I gasp for air but nothing goes to my lungs. I tense my neck and grab his arms. I try to pull his arms off me, but his body just comes closer. I have no other option but to fly up. I hover above the ship with the guard still holding onto me by the neck, suffocating me.

The guard cries out, "What the hell?" looking down as our feet dangle with the ship below us.

I try to pull his hands off of my neck, but I can't get a good grip. The guard pulls one arm back and continues to choke me with the other as he reaches for his belt. Then, I hear a gunshot.

I feel the force of the bullet pass behind me and kill the man struggling with me. I look down at the pier and see the outline of Adam's men. With my echolocation, I can zoom in for a closer look; I see Adam holding a sniper rifle. He just saved my life. At first, I am thankful. Then, I realize the man who tried to fight with me is now a corpse hanging on my back.

I let go of the dead body and watch him fall onto one of the shipping containers. I certainly wouldn't have preferred he killed me, but I didn't want him to die. If I fought better I could have taken the guard out without Adam needing to interfere. That man is dead because of me.

The three final guards all wearing the same midnight blue button-up shirts and baseball hats all gather on top of the crate and look at the dead guard. They stand pointing flashlights at his corpse, and then shine them up on me.

I point my feet toward the ground and fly down toward them as if performing a pencil dive. When I get close, I front kick one of them in the chest, pushing him to the end of the crate. He slides across the metal container and grips the edge tight as to not fall off.

As I land on the top of the metal container the other two guards aim handguns at me. The two men stand side by side in front of me. I grab one by his gun and throw him into the other guard. The two men fall off the crate and onto the bottom deck of the ship.

The first guard I kicked to the ground stands back up. I kick him with my left foot, but he ducks under it and pivots around me. I turn to face him as smacks me across the face with his flashlight.

The force pushes me off the crate. My body leaves the structure and I look down at the ten-foot drop. I use my flight and hover in the air as if I was still standing on the crate. I hover back over the crate and grab the final guard by his neck. I fly up a little higher, still holding him. Cocking my arm past my shoulder, I drag him back, and throw the final guard down.

The man's body hits the crate and tears through the metal structure. I look into the hole he makes. I don't see any guns. I fly down to the crate, tear off the metal door, and throw it across the boat. I walk into the container and search through the cargo. I tear open a box to find cans of chicken noodle soup. The cargo is completely made up of a variety of different canned foods.

I fly to different containers, and all I find are canned foods. There are no guns anywhere. Why the hell did Adam want to blow up a shipment of food? Why did he lie to me? It's time to ask him myself.

I set the bomb with a three-minute timer and drop it into the container. I throw each of the guards towards the lifeboat escaping with the bridge crew. Then I fly back to the pier. In a focused rage, I reach the pier with Adam and his militia. I see a smile on his face at first, which quickly turns into a dissatisfied scowl when I tackle him. I clench my fingers into the coarse fabric of his jacket and make a U-turn.

I fly us back to the boat while Adam struggles to escape my grip. He gives up on escaping and holds tight onto my arms in a controlling manner. I fly the two of us in between two shipping containers and I throw him into one. I look at the dent his back creates in the steel container and it reminds me of when I threw Trey through a locker last week. I continue using the force of my flight and land on top of Adam, driving my knee into his chest.

I grab him by the collar and yell, "What the hell is this Adam?"

I punch my hand through the crate and tear out a box. "These aren't guns. It's food Adam, not weapons."

"I wanted to diminish provisions during the siege," Adam explains.

"What?" I say confused.

"I was going to have to do this eventually," Adam says to himself. "I'll tell you the truth, Patrick" He looks at me in the eye.

"You're damn right. Talk!"

"Patrick, I told you my mission was to save the human race. That was a lie, and the only one I ever told you. This species has failed. They have had more than enough time to learn from their mistakes, yet they continue to make the same ones over and over again. It's insanity! Now is the time to end their path of turmoil."

"You psycho. You actually think you can destroy the human race."

"I *will* destroy them. And I'm not going to do it alone."

"Yeah, I heard your conversation with General Barringer."

"I'm not talking about Barringer—I'm talking about you Patrick. You're going to help me."

"Why would I help you? That's not just genocide—It's suicide. Why would I kill the people I love for you?"

"Because they are impulsive apes, with a need for violence engrained into their DNA. But, you will live."

"Why me?" I ask as I let go of Adam. We circle around each other as we continue to talk.

"Not just you, Patrick. We will wipe out the human population, but all superhumans will be allowed to live. General Barringer has agreed to provide our people with a sanctuary on Regnum 4. Arbitron will build us whatever we need to start over, and you and I will lead our people."

"Our people? You have powers, too?"

"We're more alike than we are different, Patrick," Adam continues, "The Nomad's will be here in a few days and when they get here—"

"Shut up! And stop talking to me like I know who these alien races are," I say to Adam. I think for a second. "You're going to help aliens invade the Earth? Tell me why you think they are so much better than us."

"The species invading the Earth is a wondering race that has lost its home planet. Their solar system's star burnt out, and now they need a new home. Their people have survived for the same amount of time as humanity and have accomplished infinitely more."

"Maybe the Nomads grew more technologically advanced in their time, but it doesn't sound to me like they've advanced in their integrity. That's the only improvement that matters. They may be united for now, but they are ready to commit genocide just to prolong their own existence!" I say to Adam. "And once they kill off the remaining humans on the planet, who's to say they don't just continue on from where we left off—on our path of 'war and destruction,' as you put it."

"You still see yourself as one of them?"

"Yes, and I am proud to be human."

"But you're not!" Adam screams.

"What have you done, Adam? How can this be undone?"

"I made my choice a long time ago. The universe is a vast, empty space. All I had to do was tell them where we are. And now they're coming."

"How can I stop this, Adam? It's not too late," I plead.

"I have devoted a great portion of my life toward killing humanity. I came closest during the Cold War. I won't let this opportunity slip away again," Adam says.

"The *NAVIGATO*," I mutter.

"You've been watching the news."

"What's your last name, Adam?" I ask, thinking back to the documents The Last Time Agent left me.

"My name," he tells me, "Is Adam Akashi."

"You were there. You worked on the *NAVIGATO* project," I go on, "You shot that woman. You almost caused a nuclear war."

"Who told you these things?"

"Adam, you tried to tear the planet apart. You say the humans are impulsive apes but we still haven't destroyed ourselves. Despite your best efforts we're still here. The mere fact that you needed an external force to destroy the human race proves that we're united."

"You'll see how fast that unity fades when the invasion begins."

"The bomb you gave me will blow up in less than a minute now. Tell me how we can call off the invasion or I will leave you here to die."

"Never gonna happen."

As Adam finishes his sentence, a helicopter flies over the boat and shines a spotlight over us. Two ropes drop down on both sides of me, thumping as they hit the steel floor of the ship. Two commandoes slide down. The two men armed with assault rifles, wearing Kevlar vests, tactical gloves, and shiny black helmets aim their weapons at my head.

I stare down Adam for a few seconds with a look of anger. I look at both commandoes who stand on each side of me. I turn to my left and grab the first commando's gun. I stare where his eyes would be if the mask didn't cover them and swiftly rip it out of his hands. The strap that attaches the gun to the man rips as I pry the weapon from his grasp.

I throw the assault rifle behind me so it knocks down the other commando. As the gun hits the commando behind me, I kick the now unarmed assailant in the center of his chest with my right foot. I turn around and swing an uppercut into the second commando's jaw and he flies up into the air. Both soldiers land on their backs.

After I neutralize the two threats, I grab Adam by the neck again and push him up against the crate.

"I'm going to kill you!"

"Good luck," Adam responds.

As Adam tells me this, about a dozen commandoes appear and take aim at me, standing atop the crates around us. The red lasers from their guns all point down at my head. I accept that I cannot win this fight. If my knuckles hurt right now from hitting people, then their bullets will certainly kill me.

I let go of Adam and fly up faster than the commandoes can aim at. They take fire, the bullets rattling as they scrape against the metal shipping containers. I'm gone before they can aim their guns into the sky. I have no idea what my next move is, but I know for a fact that I need help. I could contact The Chimaera…. No. What I need now is advice from someone I'm certain I can trust. I start heading to Dan's apartment.

1:30 A.M.

I land on the balcony of Dan's apartment and open the unlocked glass door into his living room. I can hear Dan's mother crying in her room. I'm sure that Daniel isn't hurt. Maybe they had an argument or something.

I sneak through Daniel's apartment and open the door to his room. As I enter the room, I see Daniel packing a suitcase.

"Danny, I'm sorry about what happened before, but I could really use your help right now."

"Pat, I can't help you. You should go," he says.

"Dan, please. I need you. I don't know what to do."

"I'm sorry, but I can't be your sidekick. I just can't sit by and watch any more. I need to feel like I'm actually making a difference myself. I'm taking the GED and enlisting."

"Enlisting?" I ask.

"I talked with my dad and a recruiter. They said I don't have to worry about finishing my last semester. I can start training right away and be up for active duty soon. Maybe some day I'll work with my dad at Blackstone."

"What?" I say, shocked.

"That's the private military group he works with."

"Why? Why are you doing this?" I ask.

"Because I feel useless! I feel like a drain on everyone's life."

"Dan, that's not true," I plead.

"Not everyone gets powers to prove they're special," he says remorsefully. "I'm not as lucky as you. You might be a hero someday, and I'll be forgotten."

"We're in this together, Dan."

"Yeah, I thought so, too. But when you joined track, you got popular. You got a little bit of power and you just forgot all about me. You tried to fix it. Then you got a *lot* more power, and you did the exact same thing!"

"Dan, it's not that simple," I try to get through to him. "This is bigger than how we get remembered. Something's—
"

"The military can train me. I don't have the powers you do, Pat, but with the things they can teach me...I can help people without needing superpowers. They can turn me into a soldier. I can be a hero too. But I'll never do anything great if I'm living here in the shadow of people like you, or my father," Dan tells me.

"Danny?"

"It's Daniel. I want you to leave, Patrick," he tells me.

I do as he says. I walk back to the balcony slowly. I put my hands on the balcony railing and look out at the city skyline. I pull my body forward and thrust myself head first over the edge.

I tumble through the air, my eyes stinging from fighting back tears and heavy from not sleeping.

I need serious help. My parents can't help me. It would take too much time to explain everything to them, and even if they did believe there was an alien invasion underway, they would just force me to go somewhere safe with them. I can't be looking out for myself right now.

This is the time that I need to step up and become the hero I always wanted to be. I stop tumbling and hold my body up, and direct my force ahead.

It's time to contact The Last Time Agent. The Chimaera is the only person I have left to turn to.

Chapter 7

Wednesday

4:00 P.M.

"You're almost done. 3...2...1," The Last Time Agent counts off.

I stop hovering in the air and fall to the ground. With sweat dripping from my head, I land on the floor. The Chimaera taught me to hover in air for eight minutes without touching the ground.

I wish I came to The Chimaera for help earlier. He's helped me to exceed my limits in ways I never could have imagined. He knows exactly how my powers work. He told me my abilities were like muscles I've never used before. The more I use them, the easier it gets and better I become.

I just hope this limited time we have spent training is enough for what is about to come.

"Tell me what the time is," The Chimaera orders.

I walk to my phone, which I left next to a bottle of water in the corner of my garage. I grab the phone and press the power button. It doesn't turn on.

"It's not working. I must have forgotten to charge it yesterday," I say to The Chimaera.

"Turn on the lights," he orders.

"Why? It's not even dark out yet."

"Just do it."

I walk to the switch and flip it. The lights do not turn on. "That's odd," I say.

"This is how it starts," The Chimaera tells me.

"Is it time to go to war?" I ask.

"We're going to fight, but a hero needs a uniform before he goes into battle."

The Chimaera takes out his gold and blue pocket watch. He presses against it and a wooden, rectangular box appears on the floor in front of him with the letter *C* engraved into the oak in gold. The Chimaera sets the box on the ground and opens it up. I see him hold up a thick, flowing piece of deep royal blue fabric. He hands the box to me and says, "Suit up."

I go to my room to change. On the way there, holding the wooden box in my arms, I run into my dad. "Son, we need to talk," he says.

"Not now, Dad, I have something important to do," I tell him.

"No, Patrick, I want to talk to you."

"I said, not now!" I yell at my father, realizing that I am far too quick to anger. Dan was completely right yesterday when he told how it felt when I pushed him away. I want to be a better person than I was, and I can start with my parents.

"Dad, I'm sorry. I...I just have something really important to do right now. When I come home, I promise we'll talk. Things are gonna be different when this is all over."

"When what's all over?" My mother says as she enters the room and gently grabs ahold of my arm.

"Stacie, I thought we agreed I was going to talk to him," my father says to my mom.

"It's too late to be worrying about crowding him. He needs both of his parents," my mom continues, holding my arm. She grabs my father's hand with her free hand.

"Patrick, something's wrong. You're hurting, and so are the people around you. Let your father and I help. A family is strongest together."

Kevin enters the room and stands next to me. He look up and asks, "What's in the box?"

"Don't worry buddy," I tell him, setting it down and crouching next to him. I grab his shoulders and say to them, "Don't go anywhere today. Stay in the house, lock the doors, and keep the lights off."

"Patrick, you're scaring us," my mother says.

"What's going to happen?" my father asks.

"Trust me. Everything will be just fine." I smile, assuring them of my confidence in the situation. "I'll have a great story to tell you when I'm finished. But you've got to let me live it first, before I can tell it."

I grab my mother's hand and gently remove it from the back of my arm. I pull her in for a hug. I hold her tight and she whispers in my ear, "Be safe."

I let go and hug my father. He holds me even tighter and speaks to me, "You're a man now, Pat. Just be the kind of man who inspires people. People like that kid looking up at you right now."

"I will," I tell him with an understanding smile. "I will."

I let go and lift up my brother. I tell him, "I'll see you soon, alright?"

"Okay, Patrick."

I set him down and pick up the wooden box. I start walking off and come to a stop. I look back and smile at my family. Then, I walk upstairs.

4:26 P.M.

I look at myself in the mirror. I easily adjust the well-fitted suit to the right comfort level. I can feel the mobility as I stretch my arms out. The texturized, ballistic nylon fabric rubs slightly coarse over my skin, but I quickly get used to it.

The light from the sun gleaming through my window shines brightly off the pure white fabric, washed subtly in gray. I pull down a soft, pearl mask over my head. I look through the balaclava-styled slit in the eyes, just like my old mask.

I pull the hood sewn into my cape over my head, connecting it to a piece of Velcro on top of the mask. I trace my fingers along the gold trim of the hood.

I reach down at my side tugging the navy-blue cape straight. A strap of fabric lingers up from the cape and flows down each of my shoulders and tucks under a gold metal plate of armor shaped into the letter C attached to the center of my chest.

The boots, gloves, and belt are the same navy-blue color as the cape. The blue belt breaks up the white between my chest and my legs. Additionally, the belt contains gold pouches for carrying things.

I like the white and blue color scheme of the suit. It reminds me of the first time I used my powers to help people. I wore a white shirt and a blue cape—well, a tablecloth to be more specific—when I went to go help at the hospital fire.

When I finish changing, I open a window and hover down to my garage. The door is already open, and I land across from The Chimaera, now wearing my new uniform. I can feel my cape flowing in the direction of the wind and look down to my side at the end of the fabric. I look up as I land on the grass below. I ask him, "What's the letter *C* for?"

"I think you already know what it stands for."

"Crusader," I say to myself with a revelation. The Chimaera nods. I continue, "How did I get my powers?"

"How you received your abilities is nowhere near as important as what you choose to do with them."

The light outside begins to fade away and darkness replaces it. The Chimaera and I both look up at the sun. The gleaming yellow circle fades away as a backlit cube rolls in front of it. The square shape rolls over the sun, blocking out its light. The sun's light grows dimmer and dimmer. Pure darkness overwhelms the Earth in a blanket—shadows steadily replace the dazzling blue sky tucking into the corners of the horizon, leaving the planet and myself longing for a sense of the normal.

More stars than ever before become visible to the naked eye. Looking up, I grow fearful. The sun always went unappreciated in my mind. My mother once told me that the sun and the moon act as a constant reminder that we are never truly alone. Without them, it looks like the Earth is truly lost in the expansive universe.

I stare at the spot up above that the sun disappears from and find a sea of emptiness. I look at the distant lights in the sky and notice that many of them are moving. This must be the beginning of the invasion.

"What's happening?" I ask The Chimaera.

"This is how it begins. The Nomads block out all of our sunlight with a massive cube shaped vessel. Adam has already taken out all electronic devices with EMPs scattered throughout the planet," The Chimaera says.

"Why?" I ask.

"The Nomads thrive in darkness," he tells me. "For the past several thousand years, their sun was in the final stages of its lifecycle. Their species adapted to living in dim to no light before they had to evacuate the planet when their sun died."

"How do we stop them?" I ask.

"The sun is so bright that the Nomad's will not be able to live under it. Their skin is weak and will not shield them from the radiation. They'll be weakened by the light, and it will kill them if exposed to it for more than a few days," The Chimaera tells me.

"So, we need to get the sun back. How do we do it?" I ask.

"That's not our job. At 5:47, Indomitus is going to destroy the star blockade. Our job is protecting this planet over the next hour while he focuses on that. He does his job and we do ours."

"Who is Indomitus?"

"You remember those files I left you on the *NAVIGATO* mission?"

"Yeah."

"When Isabelle Thompson launched the *NAVIGATO* into overdrive, it tore a hole in space. The *NAVIGATO* slipped through. Lieutenant Colonel Richard Wilde was launched into a transdimension where he was exposed to tremendous amounts of a rare form of radiation called the Omega. That's the source of power for superhumans. He escaped before his body started to decay and wound up in another galaxy. He was enlisted into the Alpha-Omega war, and basically won the conflict single-handedly. That's where he earned his title. He's been journeying home for nearly fifty years since then."

"I still feel like I'm missing something."

"You don't need to worry about Richard. Your job is to stop Adam," The Chimaera says. "He's the one responsible for this."

"Why do you care so much about helping me stop him?"

"I call myself The Last Time Agent. I went up against Adam in a different time and he killed every single member of my team. When it was all over, I felt lost. The Crusader made me into who I am. Today, I get to do my part and make you into the hero you're destined to become. Adam has evolved into pure evil. But evil doesn't define who we are. We can choose to be heroes."

"How was he there?" I ask, "During the *NAVIGATO* mission? He's not old enough."

"You'll find out soon," The Chimaera tells me, "It's time to fight. Are you ready?"

"Take me to Adam."

The Chimaera puts his hand on my shoulder and takes out his pocket watch.

"Close your eyes. Most people throw up if they teleport with their eyes open. The sudden change in scenery doesn't feel good."

I shut my eyes. The Chimaera clicks a button on his pocket watch and teleports us away. Then, I hear his strong, robotic voice say, "We're here," with the sound resonating from within his helmet.

We now stand at the bottom of Adam's building in downtown Chicago. It's impossible to see without the sun, and now the moon has vanished as well. The blockade probably blocks the path of light from the sun to the moon, which is why it isn't reflecting any light.

I use my echolocation to maneuver around. The Chimaera appears unaltered by the lack of sunlight. His visor most likely gives him some sort of night vision. Surprisingly, Adam's EMP hasn't affected The Chimaera's suit and his technology.

I hear people running through the streets of the city, crying out as cars pile up in the darkness. I sense several large spaceships flying between the buildings that make up Chicago's skyline. I can feel the temperature slowly dropping and I shiver. The Chimaera and I look up to the top of Adam's building.

"Give me a boost." The Chimaera orders.

I grab him and throw him up in the air. Then, I bend my legs and spring up into the air as well, quickly reaching him. The Chimaera retracts his cape and flies up the building with me. We reach Adam's floor. The Chimaera and I smash through the glass windows to enter the building. He rolls across the floor into a combat stance. I land much more gracefully on my feet, because I can control my flight path in a way that he cannot.

We stand in the hallway that leads from Adam's private elevator to his office. I sense six men armed with assault rifles lined up against the walls leading to the tall glass doors that separate the hallway from Adam's office. The crimson glow from The Chimaera's suit acts as the only reliable source of light.

I reminisce back to the first time I walked through these doors and the amazement I felt. I never imagined in that moment I would return as Adam's enemy.

I walk ahead towards the guards. I grab the closest one by the end of his rifle and throw him into the next closest guard. Another guard charges at me, and I instinctively react by kicking out and thrusting my body into his chest. He lets out a shriek as he flies through the air and crashes into a wall.

With my echolocation, I can sense The Chimaera fighting the rest. The guards open fire. The muzzles from their weapons create a second source of light in the room, similar to a strobe light in a haunted house or a night club. The red glow from The Chimaera's suit remains consistent. The bullets ricochet off of The Chimaera's armor and fall to the ground.

The Chimaera jumps at one guard, teleports behind him, and kicks him in the back of his head. A guard now standing behind The Chimaera flings a right hook at him. The Chimaera turns around and blocks it with his right hand. He then places the man's wrist into a joint lock. The Chimaera twists the man's arm and hunches him over. Once the guard loses all balance, The Chimaera sweeps the guard's leg with his left foot, kicking it up into the air. As the guard's body bounces off of the ground, The Chimaera punches him in the head and slams him back down to the carpeted floor.

The last guard creeps up to The Chimaera and presses the end of his assault rifle against The Last Time Agent's helmet. He jolts his head to the right, and the guard pulls the trigger. Bullets fly past his head, and The Chimaera knocks the gun out of his hand.

The now unarmed guard tries to kick The Chimaera, but he grabs his foot and lifts him in the air. Once the guard's head is closer to the ground than his foot, The Chimaera teleports behind him, reaches his arm around the guard's neck, and slams the back of the man's head into the ground. The impact lets out a heavy cracking sound.

The Chimaera stands up and walks toward Adam's office. He stops at the glass doors and looks inside, waiting for me. I walk next to him and give him a nod of the head. The Chimaera presses against his neck and the cape retracts back into his armor. We kick the door down to the ground. The glass shatters as the frame falls.

We enter the office with shattered chunks of glass crackling beneath our feet. Several dozen candles light up the room. Every candle has an identical, tiny, shaking flame inside.

Adam stands with his back to us, gazing outside his window. Missiles shoot down from space, buildings collapse, and people run mad in the streets. The buildings that are on fire provide barley enough light to witness the chaos.

Because of Adam's EMP's, no one can see more than a few feet ahead and cannot escape the city. They must be stricken with such fear that they won't be able to tell if their fellow man is actually an invader from another world trying to take control of the planet.

When I used to play baseball as a kid, my father told me that the team that wants it more would win the game. If that's true, I'm not really sure what race Earth will belong to when this is all over. Both the Nomads and Humanity fight for a home world.

Adam continues to look out the window and he addresses me,

"Hello, Patrick. I knew you would come, but I didn't know you would bring a friend. I don't think we've met yet."

"We've met, Adam," The Chimaera says.

"We're here to stop you," I say to Adam.

"You can't stop me," Adam says as he turns around. "No one's been able to so far."

"I guess we'll be the first," I tell Adam.

"You don't even understand how powerful I am. No one has ever stopped me. Everyone who ever got in my way has regretted it."

"What happened to you that was so bad, it caused you to do this? I can't imagine what makes a man want to commit genocide on his entire race."

"It's a very human thing, to think you're the most special person on your little world. But, I told you that you're not the only one with power, Patrick."

"What's your power?" I ask.

"Do you know how old I am, Pat?" Adam asks. I don't know the answer, but he looks like he's in his mid-forties.

"How old?"

"The greatest human minds have dated *Homo sapiens* to first appearing around two hundred thousand years ago. I've been called many names by many cultures: Wurugag...Pangu...Adam. They all mean the same thing."

"You're the first human?" I ask.

"That's right, Patrick. I am the first man," Adam tells me.

"You've lived through all of human history?" I ask.

"I have seen everything. I've seen so much pain, so much suffering. Did you know I was there when they crucified

Jesus? Humans love heroes, but they love seeing their tragic deaths even more." Adam remarks, "I've seen so much war and so much death. I've seen so much evil—and I mean true evil. Do you understand now why I want them to die?"

"No," I tell him.

"And you never will."

"Why did you use me?"

Adam starts to untie the gold necktie from his black collared shirt. He responds to me, "What I hate more than anything else in my life is that I used to think I was alone. I spent so much time looking for someone like me and always came up short. That's why I was excited to find you, Patrick. When I found another person with powers, I had to befriend you. I was suddenly not alone anymore. You inspired me to seek the rest of us out."

Adam continues, "It's kind of funny—I'm not just the first human. I'm the first *super*human."

"So, you never needed me?" I ask.

"Did you really think I needed you? I have endless resources at my disposal. I could have done all this without you. And I did," he insults me. "I let you help me as a favor. I wanted to be allies with you. We still could be allies."

"I'll never help you again, Adam," I tell him.

"That's what I thought. I think we're finished now, Patrick."

Adam wraps his necktie around his right hand for padding. He reaches into his desk and takes out an oblong black can with a metal clip at the end. Adam throws the weapon at us. The flash bang hits the ground in front of The Chimaera and me, and it releases a shriek of noise accompanied by a violent burst of light and smoke. The Chimaera seems unaffected, but I crouch down to my knees holding my burning eyes.

I can still see everything with my echolocation, but my other senses go crazy. The ringing still vibrates in my ears and I wobble around like I'm about to fall over.

I couldn't see where he found it, but Adam charges at The Chimaera with an automatic pistol. The force of the bullets push my ally back, and they start scraping the paint off his armor, revealing scratches of silver under the metallic black surface layer of paint.

Adam pins The Chimaera down to the floor, unloading the bullets into his helmet. The Chimaera's head bounces off the ground. When Adam runs out of ammo, he drops the guns and stands above The Chimaera, who still lies on the ground in pain.

Adam stares me down as I recover from the flash bang. He walks intimidatingly towards me. I see emotions of rage and hatred as Adam lunges at me in frenzy. His nostrils flare, and his lips pierce together in a square shape. We used to look at each other like father and son. Now, we're enemies.

Adam reaches me, and out of fear I throw a right punch, but he quickly blocks it. Adam switches with ease from a block to a joint lock around my right wrist. He hits me in the face with his right hand while still holding onto the left. Grabbing the back of my head, he holds on to my hood tightly. I feel trapped in this position, grappling with my former mentor. Adam drives his knee into my stomach and throws me down behind him.

As I stand up, The Chimaera charges at Adam, screaming out with his resonating voice. The Chimaera kicks at Adam, but he jumps and kicks the foot out of the way and throws a punch at The Chimaera's head. The Chimaera slips the punch and grabs Adam's arm with both hands. The Chimaera uses Adam's arm as leverage to throw him against the wall.

Adam slams into the wall and The Chimaera prepares to punch him. Adam turns out of the way and lets The Chimaera's fist penetrate the drywall. Then, he grabs two samurai swords that hang parallel to each other on the wall and holds one in each hand.

The Chimaera and I charge at Adam together. The Last Time Agent grabs a wooden bow from a shelf on the wall and yanks out a bronze arrow from an adjacent quiver. The quiver and the rest of the arrows pile to the floor and are crushed under The Chimaera's foot.

The Chimaera leaps into the air and skillfully draws back the arrow and fires it at Adam. The bronze arrow cuts the side of Adam's head, barely grazing the skin. The Chimaera lands and swings the bow at Adam, who ducks the attack. The Chimaera swings the bow back and cracks it in half over Adam's leg. Adam lets out a scream as he falls forward.

Adam now kneels on the floor between The Chimaera and me. He lunges up with a battle cry and swings both swords together from his right side to mine. I jump back to dodge them. Adam swings one sword at me again. As a reflex, I put up my right hand to block. I made the wrong decision as my arm from wrist to elbow gets sliced open.

THE CRUSADER

The ballistic nylon material protects me for the most part, but blood under my sleeve begins to seep through the fabric. Infuriated after Adam cuts me, I take the offensive. Adam swings the sword in his opposite hand at me. I duck and rise up, punching him in the chest. Adam flies backwards. He almost hits The Chimaera, who teleports out of the way. Adam hits the wall at the end of the room and makes a dent in it before he falls to the ground. He seems to be unconscious.

The Chimaera and I walk towards Adam. When we get close, Adam places his hand on a panel attached to the wall. I hear a beeping sound from the wall as a section of it slides open into a door shaped opening, similar to an elevator. Adam dives into the hidden chamber, which remains out of my line of sight.

The Chimaera runs into the room. From where I stand, I'm still unable to see the inside. However, I can see white paneling lining the walls of the room. I run ahead, about to enter, when The Chimaera flies out landing on his back with a crack in his visor.

Adam walks out of the room pumping a shotgun. The Chimaera would have been dead without his helmet. Adam continues shooting The Chimaera on the ground.

The Chimaera teleports to Adam's side and tears the metal rifle out of his hands. He cracks the shotgun in half over his knee and whacks Adam in the head with one of the pieces.

Adam falls to the ground and looks at the samurai swords he dropped earlier. Adam crawls ahead quickly to grab them.

I race over to the other side of the room. Adam stands up and swings at The Chimaera. The sword cracks in half as it hits The Chimaera's blocking hand like a fragile baseball bat. The Chimaera lowers his hand slowly, knowing he has gained the upper hand, and kicks Adam in his knee. Adam slides down to his right, holding himself up on an angle against the nearby wall.

The Chimaera follows up with a right straight punch. Adam jerks his head to the side and The Chimaera's fist smashes through the wall. Adam steps closer to The Chimaera, grabs his helmet, and smashes his head into the wall.

The Chimaera teleports to Adam's left and punches him in the throat. He grabs Adam by the hair on his head and pulls it back. The Chimaera prepares to smash his head into the wall. Adam barely escapes The Chimaera's hold and the two begin to wrestle, alternating joint locks.

I clench my fingers into his shoulders and yank him down as I drive my left knee into his spine. Adam lets out a gasp and a shriek, and I throw him off The Chimaera. Adam flies across the room and lands on top of his desk, cracking it in half.

The Chimaera and I walk over to Adam. I pick him up by his collar and pull him close as I headbutt him. I elbow him in the face, then punch him. Adam smiles showing his dark blood seeping in the gaps between his teeth.

I let go of him, knowing he won't be a problem anymore. I crouch down next to him over the shattered remnants of his desk and say,

"Adam, call the Nomads and tell them to retreat."

"Not even I can stop this now." He tells me.

Adam slams his head into mine. He tries to stand up but is only able to get on his knees before The Chimaera grabs him by the neck and throws him through the window. The

Chimaera holds Adam up by the neck hanging out over the city. The Last Time Agent speaks,

"I've got this, Crusader. You need to get out there and help whoever you can."

"How will we stay in contact?" I ask.

"I saw some radios in Adam's arsenal," The Chimaera tells me.

I fly into the arsenal in the corner of the room and grab the radios. The Chimaera throws Adam to the ground and kicks him. The Chimaera takes the radios from me and attaches two thin, circular devices to them from his armor. He sticks them to each radio and tells me,

"These should work. Now go out there and help."

I run to the smashed window, the one that The Chimaera broke with Adam's body. I walk out the gap and begin hovering outside.

I drift in the air and look back inside the building. The Chimaera holds up Adam and begins hitting him over and over again. The Chimaera starts yelling, "You killed them! You killed all of them!"

"Who are you talking about?" Adam asks.

"You haven't done it yet, but you will. I don't care what point in time it happens—I want my revenge now!"

Adam is going to kill some people very close to The Chimaera in the future. Of course, that means Adam is going to make it through this alive. Adam told me he was the first human, but he didn't say what his power was. Could he reincarnate himself or could he just heal? It doesn't matter anymore, because we stopped him. After this is all over, I can worry about sending him to prison, but, for now, I need to protect people from these alien invaders. I have no idea what the Nomads look like. They may look just like us, or they may look like monsters. Maybe we look like monsters to them.

Darkness spreads and the temperature rapidly drops without the sun. I sense the particles of my breath freeze as they pass through my mask. A dozen relatively small spaceships soar through the city firing missiles at people and buildings.

I fly at one of the midnight-jade ships and ram into it with my shoulder, forming more of a dent in my arm than the ship itself. The spacecraft is oblong in the center, with sprawling wings on the sides, making the vessel look like a crow. I rub my hands across the metal. I can feel a texture like moss as I brush my fingers across the ship's hull.

I hang onto the side of the ship and start smashing my hand down on it with a hammer-like fist. My hand quickly starts aching, so I give up the pointless attempts at fighting it.

I hear the engines roaring around me, like the runway of an airport. The deep sound resonates, surrounding the area as four more crow-like Nomad ships surround me.

I hear a crackling noise emitted from the ship's speakers. Are the aliens trying to communicate with me in their language? I don't understand. It sounds like Arabic or Mandarin, or maybe a mix of the two. Unfortunately, their dialect has no similarities to French, the one foreign language I studied in school.

From context, the aliens are probably telling me to surrender. I don't want to surrender, but I can't think of an alternative. I know they will probably kill me before I even touch them, but I prepare to fly at one of the ships.

Then, everything changes. I raise my hand to shield the sun from my eyes. I'm only annoyed for a second before I realize what this means, and I regain a sense of hope.

The sunlight blinds me. It is so much brighter than I remember. The blockade covering the star passes like an eclipse and the complete radiance of the sun returns. Seeing that star again makes me smile. I see a square-shaped object position over the sun and shrink as it gets closer. It looks as though the Nomad's sun blockade flew into the sun and burnt up.

The obstruction fully disappears, and the sun returns in all its glory. This must have been what The Chimaera was talking about when he said that Indomitus would take care of the blockade.

Fighting off the Nomad's should be easier with the sun on my side. The very thing that gives hope to this world strikes terror in theirs. The sunlight will drive them off the planet soon.

I see a spaceship unlike any of the Nomad's flying towards me. The ship seems human and bears the title *U.S.S NAVIGATO* on it. The Chimaera talked about Indomitus like he was very powerful, but how powerful could he be?

The *NAVIGATO* flies in at one of the four surrounding ships, exhausting a unique lemon medallion and iris flame for propulsion. The *NAVIGATO* fires a missile at one ship, creating an explosion larger than I have ever seen. It lands at the end of the line of Nomad ships. Out from the back hatch of the ship, a man wearing black and red flies out.

This must be Indomitus. He flies down the line of ships. His hands begin to glow bright like the sun. Lasers the color of a fiery marigold expel from his arms out towards the Nomad ships. The energy beams strike the first ship and after several seconds, chunks of the black and jade metal fly out of an overwhelming exhaust of flame.

Indomitus fires his lasers at the third ship. I measure the strength of his blast by the color of the beam; it's not as luminous, so it must be weaker.

Before the Nomad ship blows up like the other two, Indomitus flies to the remaining ship. He grabs the massive vessel with both arms and throws it into the other ship. Both ships explode, and Indomitus escapes the massive ball of flame hovering in the sky above Chicago.

The power of Indomitus leaves me in complete awe. After he finishes saving me from the Nomad ships, Indomitus flies on top of the crow-styled ship I'm still hanging on. I fly up and stand next to him.

Indomitus stands a few inches taller than me, with the posture of a military man and looks me straight in the eye. The man has brown hair and stubble growing on his face. His uniform is mostly black. His boots and gloves are gray, and the borders of these items are highlighted in red.

The fabric on his shoulders and neck are washed dark gray and in the center of his chest is a line that shoots down his torso to his metal belt. The belt is outlined in a red garnet as well, just like every other section of the suit that is gray.

This line connected to his belt and upper chest creates the abstract outline of the letter *I*. The gray areas all lie over a black jumpsuit, with patches and folds like an air force pilot uniform.

I look down at the ship we stand on top of. Indomitus extends out his hands and aims the tips of his finger at the hull of the ship. His hands and forearms begin to glow with the same fiery light as before. Indomitus fires lasers at the ship's exterior and cuts out the outline of a circle. He stomps his leg down on the circled area, and the plate of the ship's hull falls into the interior. Indomitus looks at me and says, "Follow me."

He jumps down the hole, and I follow him in. We both hover down so our feet land on the floor of the ship. I can barely contemplate my surroundings. This is nothing like I would expect an alien ship to look like

from the way they are in movies. The lack of light makes it difficult to see. Luckily, I don't need to see.

I sense several computer monitors built into the walls, which release a remarkably dim light. It's nearly impossible to see the aliens because of the lack of light they live in. The ship itself is just like the outside, made of a dark, military green and midnight jade stone.

Two soldiers stand from their seats in what I believe to be the cockpit. They stand up wearing dark green uniforms with black armor. They wear simple black helmets with yellow lights gleaming like chilling, shimmering eyes. The perfect gold circles resemble the eyes of a demon.

The two pilots take out their sidearms, which appear to be handheld laser guns. Their weapons are a dark and rusted gold. The weapons start pulsing green with energy.

Indomitus waves his hands up gracefully, and the guns fly out of the alien's hands and hit the ceiling. He then outstretches his arms, aiming one hand at each soldier and waves them to the side. The aliens follow the path of Indomitus' hands and fly into the sides of the ship.

Indomitus walks ahead to the front of the ship where the two pilots sat. Another alien soldier charges from behind with a battle cry. Once I sense him, I turn quickly stretching out my arm and strike him with a backfist. My knuckles crack through his helmet like glass. The glowing yellow eyes fade out and the Nomad soldier falls straight to the ground.

I look back to Indomitus at the main console. He presses some buttons on the ship's computers and adjusts a hand crank protruding from the hull of the ship. When he finishes, he zaps the controls with a laser from his right hand. The computer begins to overheat and smokes. Indomitus says to me,

"Get off the ship."

Indomitus flies through the wall of the ship and I follow him through the crater his body forms. I catch up to him and hear the ship explode behind us. We both hover in the air over a street and in between two buildings.

"So, you can fly, too?"

"Yeah…I used to think I was the only one with powers," I tell him.

"So did I. But I guess we're never truly alone, are we?" Indomitus says with a calming smile.

THE CRUSADER

"I guess you're right," I tell him.

"How did you get your powers?"

"I don't really know. All I remember is a lot of smoke and a blinding green light."

"Interesting," he remarks.

"How did you get yours?" I ask.

"It's a very long story," he says. "What's your name?"

"Patrick. Patrick Knight"

"Wrong answer. A hero needs a name. A title that others can call them. Your title can't be an ordinary name or else it looses the effect. People won't remember the name Richard Wilde, but they will remember Indomitus. That's what people call me."

"Why Indomitus?"

"I was given the title during the Alpha-Omega War by people from the planet Regnum 4. It has the same meaning in most places."

"What's that?" I ask.

"On most planets beyond our system, it means hero or savior. Hopefully after today, Earth will agree. You wear the letter *C* on your chest. That must mean something."

"It stands for Crusader."

"I like it. The Crusades were fighters in the Holy Wars. Nothing is more personal than religion. That shows your mission to save people is personal. It's your crusade. That's a good name."

"Thank you. So, um, what *are* your powers?

"I usually have a power for any situation. It get's kind of boring." Indomitus says.

"Oh, I'm sure you keep things interesting." I say.

"I'm discovering new powers all the time. It should be the same for you."

"So, what do we do now?" I ask.

"I have a fleet of ships in orbit taking the Nomad's main force head on. The battle will be over soon, but, until then, we need to control the invading army down here. These Nomads don't have a standard chain of command—they follow the strongest. The largest force is located in London. That's where I'm going now."

"What about me?"

"Stay here, Crusader. This is your home. You know the terrain better than the Nomads, so fight them off your turf."

"I assume this is the last time we'll meet then."

"I wouldn't be so certain of anything."

Indomitus flies back to his ship. He enters the *NAVIGATO* through the back hatch. The hatch closes behind him and the *NAVIGATO* flies up.

I watch the ship fly up past the sun, in awe of meeting a man of such power. Meeting Indomitus was like meeting a celebrity. Flying with someone else helped ease the feeling of loneliness plaguing me since I first discovered my abilities.

6:15 P.M.

My radio begins to screech with static and background noise. I withdraw the radio from my belt and hold it against my ear.

"Chimaera, what's going on?" I answer.

"Hello, Patrick," says the indistinguishable voice of Adam.

"Adam! What did you do to The Chimaera?" I ask.

"Don't worry about him. He's not the one who needs your help right now."

"What have you done?"

"You should have protected your family, Patrick. Now, go home." What could Adam have done to my family? I drop the radio and fly home faster than I have ever flown before.

NICHOLAS CHIMERA

Chapter 8

6:50 P.M.

I fly back to my neighborhood with no difficulty locating my house. I can see the smoke of the burning building miles away.

I land on my front lawn and sprint up the cement path to my house. Flames engulf my home, tearing apart the roof and releasing dark smoke through a few open windows and the front doorway, which has been broken through. I race through the doorway and stomp over the cracked white door.

Both of my parents are on the floor of my living room. I run to my mother. At first, I don't recognize her because the flames have charred her skin. I remember the fire at the hospital when I watched the nurse die in front of me. No one deserves this.

I tear off my cape and the hood attached to it and use it to smother the flames over her. Once the fire is out, I pick her up and fly out the windows in the front of the house. When I reach the window, I turn my back to it so the glass doesn't hurt her. I crash through and land on the front lawn. I set my mother down in the grass. I press my finger first against her neck and then her wrist, searching for a pulse—I feel nothing. I hold my hands over her body, shaking and not sure what to do. My echolocation can't sense a heartbeat...

She's dead.

I fly in after my dad. I bend down next to him and see a tiny, lead bullet casing on the ground. I look down and see a bullet hole through his leg. Adam's men must have shot his leg so he couldn't escape the fire. I lift up my father and fly him outside, setting him down next to my mother.

Half of his face is completely burnt. He's still alive but in so much pain. I've never heard my father cry out with such anguish in my life. I hold him in my arms and tear off my mask so he knows it's me. He begins to choke, crying as he sees my mother, and calls out my name, "Patrick..."

"Don't talk, Dad. Save your energy. I'm so sorry for everything. I treated you and mom horribly this past week. I—"

"I...I want you to know...I understand. I want you to..."

A bullet suddenly fires, piercing through my father's skull. His blood splatters onto my costume, undoubtedly leaving a noticeable stain over what used to be clean white. I set his body down and wipe his blood from my face. The blood stains my gloves as well. I take them off and throw them to the ground.

I let loose a series of sounds, moans, and cries. The random grouping of syllables is impossible to control. My hands shake and my throat goes dry. I quickly lose my ability to see once fought tears clog my eyelids. At first, I open my eyes wider. Then, I close them. By shutting my eyelids, the pressure squeezes the tears out through my eyelashes.

Out of instinct, I sense where the bullet came from with my echolocation. A sniper stands on the roof of the apartment complex across from my house. I broke my leg trying to jump to the roof of this building a week ago.

I race across the street, snarling. I wildly flail my arms, bouncing from side to side as I dodge the bullets that crack into the cement street at my sides. I cross the street, and the bullets begin tearing up the grass, shooting dirt into the air coating my legs.

I fly at the sniper, ready to punch a hole through his stomach. I land next to him on the roof with ease, and reach my hands out to grab him as he pulls out a pistol. I expect him to aim the gun at me, but he pushes it up against his head and pulls the trigger.

I wanted to murder the sniper for what he did. I recognize the sniper as one of the men who used to pick me up and drive me downtown to Adam's office. Adam knew I would want to kill him, and he purposefully ordered this man to kill himself to agitate me. Either that, or the sniper knew how powerful I was, and thought a bullet in the head would be better than my arm through his chest.

Adam's the one who deserves to die. I hear the static of a radio and check my own. I look down and see that the sniper has a radio on his belt, which goes off now. I drop my radio to the ground and pick up the snipers. Adam's voice comes through.

"I'm on top of the Sears Tower, Patrick. Get over here if you want to see your little brother again."

The death of my mother and father made me forget all about Kevin. I won't let him die like our parents.

7:30 P.M.

I stand on top of the Sears Tower. I can see the sun naturally setting now. One by one, the ships in orbit fly off. The aliens in Chicago retreat along with the rest of their race. The invasion is finished—the Nomads failed. The only thing left to do is to punish Adam.

I stand on the roof, my arms and legs trembling. I'm not sure if it's due to anger or physical exhaustion. I look around the city at collapsed buildings, noticing the countless cars piled under bridges and overpasses. When the sun returned, the first responders went to work putting out the fires and getting people to hospitals. They still have plenty of work to do. As much I want to help out now, I need to stop the man responsible for this. I need vengeance, and the tangible incarnation of that vengeance is on this roof, standing across from me.

Adam holds my little brother with a gun to his head and an arm around his throat. The Chimaera lays at his feet with a sword through his chest. The Last Time Agent's helmet has been torn off, leaving the man underneath the armor exposed with loose wires and metal chunks arranged around the armor in his neck. The Chimaera's face is scarred and tired. He has black hair with gray temples.

The Last Time Agent is still alive. My brother is still alive. Adam is still alive—but I am going to change that right now. I wipe a fresh tear from my eye and blink rapidly as dirt and blood seeps into my eye. Adam says to me, "Stay right there, Patrick! You can't move faster than a bullet."

"I'm going to kill you!" I scream at him, clothed in the dirty remains of my costume. Not only are parts of it missing, left next to my parent's bodies at home, but the clean white colors of the suit are degraded and turned dark by the dirt and smog from the fire. On it, there are splashes of murky blood from my parents and my own wounds.

"I can't be killed. You know how old I am."

"I'm going to murder you, Adam," I say with conviction.

"You still don't fully understand how my powers work, Patrick. My lifespan isn't just infinite. I cannot be killed.

Something always gets in the way. Shoot me and the gun will jam. Stab me and the sword will crack. Some miracle always gets in the way."

"Why did you kill my parents? Why are you trying to kill my brother? Why are you doing this?"

"Because I hate you, Patrick Knight! The only thing that mattered to me was my mission, and you stopped it. So now, I'm going to take away what matters to you most."

"I didn't stop this. I tried to, but Indomitus was the one who stopped the invasion. He's the one who got in your way." I plead.

"He'll get what's coming too. But, you. I hate you for trying. I hate you for betraying me," Adam tells me. "Here's a lesson for you that I learned a long time ago: Don't care about people. Your enemies will only use them against you. Loved one's only get in the way of what needs to be done."

Adam throws my brother off the roof of the building. I have to act now. I fly at Adam and tackle him off the roof. I grip his body tight, trying to crush him. I look down over his shoulder at the cement over a thousand feet below. I fly down at my brother, still holding Adam in my arms. When I get close to Kevin, I drop Adam and reach for my little brother.

Adam tumbles past my brother, down toward the ground. I lose track of how close we are to the base of the skyscraper, listening to the wind whistle past our bodies tumbling down the building to the street down below. I grab onto Kevin and pull him close to me as Adam falls further away from us. I try to slow down, unable to ignore the adrenaline rush from falling.

We're going to hit something—the cement is too close now. I rotate my body and turn my back so it faces the ground. I hit the street and fall on top of a car, shattering the windshield.

I only survive the fall because my flight slowed us down enough to limit the force pulling us towards death. I hold my brother tight and thank God he is okay. I set him down on the sidewalk and pant heavily. I gasp for air and cry out at the pain shooting up my back. I roll off the car, crashing down onto my arms.

I catch my breath and push myself up. I look at Adam, who lies on the ground bleeding from his head. His back has bent nearly ninety degrees in the wrong direction. He's hurt, but the problem is, I can still hear his heart beating. I can see people running through the rubble that coats the streets of the city. They scatter searching for a way to their loved ones. I listen to the sound of sirens in the distance, Chicago's finest looking to help the people injured by the invasion.

I look back at Adam, and my temper grows knowing he was responsible for the destruction of my city and cities all over the world. Every single person who was injured or killed deserves justice for what this monster did.

The Chimaera appears next to me. "You can't kill him," he says. Not yet."

"Why not?" I ask.

"Because it can't be done. You don't have the right tools to kill him yet, but trust me. Eventually, he is going to die," The Chimaera says.

"When?" I ask.

"I can't tell you that. I can tell you he's paralyzed. He's going to rot in prison until he heals, and that will be much longer than you think. Once he does heal, he'll start planning, and he'll come after us with everything he's got. You and I will go to war with him, and we win. Of course, we never feel like we win."

"Why can't you just give me what I need to kill him now?"

"Despite the terrible things he is still going to do, it's necessary. If he doesn't do the things he does in the future, then neither of us will become heroes. A lot more people would die if we killed him. It's hard to accept, but sometimes you just need to let history take its course. Let the terrible times pass so the good ones can flourish."

"So we just leave him here?"

"Exactly. Walk away. Let him rot. Someone will come along and bring him to a hospital. They'll find out who he is and that he was responsible for deploying the EMP's. Adam didn't work very hard to cover up his crimes because he was certain he would win."

I look at The Last Time Agent. He looks me in the eye, saying, "Trust me. Just Walk away."

I look at Adam, lying on the cracked cement in anguish with a broken spine. I look down on him saying, "Maybe you're better off this way." I turn my back to him. I look up shutting my eyes. I open them asking, "What am I supposed to do now?"

"Keep being a hero. Find others like you with powers and work with them. There's a lot more people like you out there than you think. Just remember that one day some people are

185

really going to need your help, and you need to believe the crazy story they tell you. I wish I could say more—I need to leave now."

"Are you leaving for good?" I ask.

"You'll be seeing me soon, Crusader," The Chimaera assures me.

The Last Time Agent takes out his pocket watch and teleports away. I have to leave before anyone can see who I am—I don't have my mask anymore. I need to repair the costume. I need to get ready.

I need to take care of Kevin. I crouch down next to my little brother and hold him tight. I whisper into his ear with tears in my eyes, "It'll be okay buddy. Let's get out of here."

I hold on to Kevin with my life and hover into the air. We rise up slow at first and then take off into the sky faster. Kevin looks down for a few seconds and gets scared. He brings his head up and tucks it into my shoulder.

I have no idea where to go. I can't bring Kevin back to the house; he wouldn't be able to handle it. I won't be able to handle it, either. I fly us several blocks down toward the Chicago River. I set us down at an empty spot near a cement staircase near a bridge. We both sit down on the cement stairs, still roughly in tact. I don't know what to say to him.

"Are you...okay?" I ask.

"What happened?" he cries.

"A lot. A lot happened."

"Where are Mommy and Papa?"

"What do you remember happening?"

"The bad men came to the house. They kicked the door down. They hurt our parents."

"Then what?"

"They dragged me into their car and drove away."

I begin to cry thinking about the news I have to tell Kevin. It'll break my heart to speak the words. I don't want to believe it's true. What do I say? Is there a better way to phrase it than, *our parents are dead?* I put my face into my palms, and the tears drip from my eyes. I drag my arms over my head and grip the back of my skull. I set my head down into my knees.

I miss my parents. I miss the days when they could hold me and tell me everything was okay. Kevin needs that right now more than I do. It's so unfair. But, I guess *I'm* the adult now. Adults have to deal with their own problems. But, not enough of them help others deal with their problems.

"Where are Mommy and Papa?"

"They're gone."

"Are we ever going to see them again?" he asks.

"Maybe one day. Maybe one day we'll all be together again. But not for a long time."

Why did they have to be taken from us? I thought I was doing what God wanted me to do. I made the change. I fought His battle—I fought for the people of this planet. I didn't do it for reward or glory. I did it for forgiveness, but after it all, I feel even guiltier.

I don't know if there is a god. I don't know if there's a plan. I know that I'm here. Right now, I am here. And right now people need me. Kevin needs a brother. And the people of this city...they need a Crusader who will fight for them. Someone to stop men like Adam. No one else was there today to stop him. I fought the man responsible for the invasion and I paid.

There's so much I don't know—so much I need to learn. I don't know who The Chimaera is. I suppose all I need to know is that he is The Last Time Agent.

I think for a second about who I am. I am Patrick Knight. But Indomitus taught me that I need to become more than just a name to be a hero. By his word, I learned that we are never truly alone. The Chimaera was there for me when I thought I had no friends left. I found an ally in a stranger from space.

My dad would have loved to hear this story. My mom would only care that Kevin and I are safe.

Despite what my parents and the allies I fought alongside taught me, I've learned my greatest lesson from my worst enemy. Adam taught me that power can change people into something they're not. I believe Adam was a good person once. His powers may have corrupted his mind over the thousands of years he possessed them. But I don't think power changes people. Power gives people the opportunity to reveal who they truly are.

I thought my powers changed me into something I wasn't when I started hurting people in the name of justice. My powers did change me at first, but that was only the first step on a path towards the revelation of my inner self. I know now that there's always time to change. There's always time to decide what we want to be.

Power is the ultimate force toward revealing what someone is really capable of. Adam proved he was capable of causing great destruction. Now, I must spend my life proving who I really am and staying true to myself.

Am I The Crusader?

Epilogue

The metal doors slide open. Patrick Knight enters the prison cell without the escort of the guards. As the doors close behind him, the light dims, returning to its previous state of darkness. Patrick stands at the foot of the bed, staring down the man who killed his parents. Adam Akashi's eyes continue to wander off, glaring at the same point on the blank walls of his cell. Patrick tries to view the crippled anarchist with pity rather than hatred. Patrick squeezes his right hand into a tight fist, but the left remains open and calm.

"It's been five years, Patrick," Adam says, confined to the bed in his paralyzed state

"I know how long it's been," Patrick responds, spiteful.

"Why are you here? To assure yourself of my misery?" Adam asks.

"Closure," Patrick states.

"There's no such thing. I destroyed you from the inside. You've thought about what happened every day since. A conversation with me won't change a thing."

"After what happened five years ago, I tried to go back to normal. My brother and I had family who treated us well. I tried going to college. I tried everything, but I couldn't be normal. Because I'm not. You said it yourself: I'm not human anymore. I'm superhuman. So I've been focusing on what I'm meant for. And I've been finding others like me. People like us."

"Forgive me if I cannot bow down before the great 'Chicago Crusader.' All hail the warrior messiah. You think yourself so righteous, flying around with that cape over your shoulders. But, I know who you really are. I've seen that look in your eyes. You're addicted to hurting others. For a little while, no one will care because you're hurting criminals. But, as soon as you make a mistake, the world will see who they need to fear. Deep down, Patrick, you're just as bad as I am."

"I've been thinking a lot about what happened. The invasion...everything that led up to it. I've been racking my brain trying to figure out why you needed me."

"I told you before, Patrick, I never needed you."

"You said that, but I don't think it's true. I can understand why you wanted to destroy the world. By now, you've done it all. You've planned to destroy the Earth for hundreds of years and in the last few centuries with new technology, you've had the means to do it. And you came so close five years ago—I wonder if you set yourself up for failure."

"What?" Adam exclaims with disgust.

"I wonder if you subconsciously didn't want to win. After living here for countless lifetimes, destroying the world is the last thing you have left to do. I think you were scared of what would happen after you won."

"Patrick, I am cursed with eternal life. I am cursed with rage. I will not stop until every living thing in the universe is dead. Maybe then, my curse can be lifted."

"And, if it doesn't, you'll still be alone."

"What you don't understand is that I have time on my side. I don't have to rush. Assuming you have a long life, in eighty years you'll be dead, and my body would have healed itself. I have a life sentence, sure, but my life will last longer than the U.S. government. I've seen many nations rise and fall. Everyone dies...except me. These walls will crumble around me, and I will still be here ready to destroy. It's not a matter of *if*, it's *when*. I will destroy this planet. I will destroy them all! The odds are on my side."

"You're a lunatic," Patrick pauses before adding, "and, you're wrong."

"How?" he yells, "Tell me how I am wrong."

"Because, Adam, no matter when you try to destroy the world, no matter what year, or what continent...there will always be someone like me there to stop you. You have become evil incarnate. You are this planet's original sin. But there will always be a hero who can stand up to you. And that hero could be anyone."

Patrick Knight walks back to the cell doors and knocks gently against the metal, with his back to Adam.

"You'll never be anything but a thug, Patrick. I made you what you are."

"And, you'll live to see what I become, watching my work from this cell."

Patrick leaves the room, turning around as the cell doors begins to shut. He stares at Adam. The paralyzed inmate makes eye contact with him, smiling while Patrick's expression is as stoic as marble.

"I guess we'll have to wait and see. Power grants opportunity, but time...time reveals all."

ABOUT THE AUTHOR

Born June 28th, 2001, **Nicholas Chimera** has always had an enthusiasm to create. Nick has used everything he has learned and injected it into his writing, particularly his martial arts background. He earned a black belt in Tae Kwan Do when he was 13 years old, and currently studies traditional Shorin Ryu Karate.

Through the Advocacy Club at his high school, Nicholas Chimera played a major role in planning and promoting an event to create and ship prosthetic hands to people all over the world plagued by the issue of landmines.

Nick Chimera began writing **The Crusader** in his freshman year at Brother Rice High School and spent the following two years perfecting the writing. It all began with an idea for the costume—all white with a blue cape and hood.

Nicholas Chimera hopes you enjoy his first book, *The Crusader*—the beginning of a vast universe of heroes and villains and the conflicts people face as they react to power.

ABOUT THE PUBLISHER

GenZ™ is an innovative publisher for the new generation to have their work seen, recognized, published, and read by millions. We are on a mission to improve the world one word at a time. That is why we are the place for voices to be heard in a way not previously done in print or on digital media.

It can be nearly impossible for young writers with promising talent to produce standout work that will be recognized, because of the state of the publishing and digital media industries. Having work recognized in a sea of so many writers is even tougher. That is why there is an underrepresentation of young and innovative voices in the publishing and print world. There are many unheard voices. GenZ™ is on a mission to change that.

GenZ™ provides a medium where these people can be positively recognized for their work through a professional product and supportive company.

Learn more about GenZ Publishing™, how you can get involved, and all of our newest releases at GenZPublishing.org. Like us on Facebook at GenZ Publishing™ and follow us on Twitter.